WHEN THE ENGLISH FALL

✕ ✕ ✕ ✕ ✕ ✕ ✕ ✕

WHEN THE
ENGLISH
FALL

✕ ✕ ✕ ✕ ✕ ✕ ✕ ✕

A NOVEL

DAVID WILLIAMS

ALGONQUIN BOOKS OF CHAPEL HILL   2017

Published by
Algonquin Books of Chapel Hill
Post Office Box 2225
Chapel Hill, North Carolina 27515-2225

a division of
Workman Publishing
225 Varick Street
New York, New York 10014

This is a work of fiction. While, as in all fiction, the literary
perceptions and insights are based on experience, all names, characters,
places, and incidents either are products of the author's imagination
or are used fictitiously.

LIBRARY OF CONGRESS
CATALOGING-IN-PUBLICATION DATA
Names: Williams, David (David Gerald), [date]–
Title: When the English fall : a novel / by David Williams.
Description: First edition. | Chapel Hill, North Carolina :
Algonquin Books of Chapel Hill, 2017.
Identifiers: LCCN 2016053909 | ISBN 9781616205225
Subjects: LCSH: Amish—Pennsylvania—Lancaster County—Fiction. |
Solar activity—Fiction. | Disasters—Fiction. | Regression (Civilization)—
Fiction. | Survival—Fiction. | Lancaster County (Pa.)—Fiction.
Classification: LCC PS3623.I556494 W47 2017 | DDC 813/.6—dc23
LC record available at https://lccn.loc.gov/2016053909

10 9 8 7 6 5 4 3 2 1
First Edition

To "Uncle Bob" Margrave,
because good English teachers make a difference.

WHEN THE ENGLISH FALL

DEPARTMENT OF THE ARMY
JOINT EMCOM REGIONAL HEADQUARTERS
U.S. ARMY WAR COLLEGE, CARLISLE BARRACKS

REPLY TO THE ATTENTION OF:

COL. T. MARKER, FACULTY INSTRUCTOR

TO: DR. J. ERNESTINE, DEPT. SOCIOLOGY, U. PENN.

SUBJECT: Diaries

Per agreed-upon material-handling protocols established at the Joint EmCom/War College/U. Penn. meeting, enclosed with this memo are a set of five leather-bound notebooks, handwritten, retrieved from an abandoned Old Order farmhouse (PA Agricultural Reclamation Zone 7). These fit the criteria for original textual documentation, per your request to EmCom and the outputs of the aforementioned meeting with Joint EmCom and War College representatives.

The point of contact for this action is the undersigned, at secmail terry.e.marker.mil@mail.mil.

Terrence E. Marker
Col., Joint EmCom
Faculty Instructor, U.S. Army War College

[attached note]

Jeanine:

Hey, it was great seeing you, and maybe when I'm up your way later in the summer I'll bring by that bottle of scotch we talked about. Glenmorangie, eighteen years old. Not much of that around anymore. I've been saving it. Special occasion, which I'm sure it'll be.

The diaries are, well, I've read them. They appear to be exactly what you told me you're looking for. The right timing, both pre- and post-event. Some odd details. See what you think.

Look forward to seeing you again. —Terry

September 2

I hold her, tight in my arms, and she screams.

It is the morning, it is dawn, and the red sun fills the bedroom with late summer heat, and as she strains I hold her tighter, and still she screams. Her eyes are wide and unseeing, and her arms lash out, a dress on a clothesline before a storm.

I feel her body, my little bird, my little Sadie, her back pressed to my chest, taut as bent wood. I feel my arms, tired from the holding. My ears ring. And still she writhes and bucks, her head casting back and forth.

This is a long one, the worst seizure in weeks. I do not know how long it has been, but it was night when the cries began, and now day has come.

Hannah was with us, for a while, but now it is morning, and there is much to be done. Jacob is helping Hannah, I am sure. The tasks of the day play across my thoughts. The horses. Preparing the field. That unfinished chair. But I cannot focus, not even enough to pray.

There are words in her screaming, and names. Some I understand, though I do not know why she calls them out.

"Danny, oh God, Danny, oh God, oh God."

I do not know a Danny.

Her voice rasps, flayed and weakened, but still she cries out. "Doe Wah Jew Say Oh! Doe Wah Jew Say Oh Han Nan Neem!" Not English, not *Deitsch*. Words with no meaning, just sounds.

And always, always, she screams that they are falling. "They fall! They fall!" And about the beautiful wings. And about the angels. It is beautiful and horrible, whatever it is she sees with those unseeing eyes.

Her voice stills, and she pants, breath rapid, in and out, in and out.

And then, just as sudden as the first cry in the night, she shudders.

Then her voice, familiar, like sand, like dust.

"Dadi?"

She turns, and her eyes are tired. "Oh, Dadi."

That was how today began. And then the labors of the day came, and I am so tired now that I can barely write. But I write just the same.

September 3

I should not be writing this tonight. That thought is in my head right now.

I should pray. I should sleep. I especially should sleep. I should not write, for it is wasteful and prideful. Or so whispers my uncle's voice, from long ago. So chides my father. His voice is stronger.

But still, I write.

It is a prideful thing, that I sit here in the faint light alone. So the echoes of my past tell me. Around me, the house is asleep, as I should be. I like the sound of it, this sleeping house. It is not empty, because even though I can barely hear it, the softness of breathing fills the house like goose feathers.

Jacob barely stirs, strong boy that he is becoming. Sadie, oh, Sadie. She sleeps well, soft and safe tonight so far, thanks be to God. I pray, O God, that she will sleep tonight.

I say that I must stay awake until my heart is stilled, and I say that I must stay awake to listen for Sadie. But Hannah knows. She knows that I need to write.

Hannah is so kind, to understand. I should be in our bed with her, and I will be. But soon.

Today was good, a blessing, like every day is a blessing. I suppose that is why I still write here, to remember the blessings. And all things are blessings, even the hard things.

Memory is why I began to write. It was why I wrote as a boy, to remember my dreams and the hopes I had. I read back those old books now, written in secret. I am still that boy, I think.

But I needed to write, too, all those years ago when I was out in the World, out among the English.

I wanted to remember, to remember what I thought and felt and knew. It was so different, amazing and terrible, and I wanted to remember. Others left with me, when the time came for our running around. Some came back. But others didn't return, not to the hard coldness of the community where we had grown up.

Atlee fell into drinking, and then he was gone. Martha, with her laugh, with that twinkle in her eye. That twinkle was gone when I last saw her, and her laugh was hard like brass. So many terrible things in the world.

And Simon. Simon had never liked the Order, never been at ease with the life of the plain. I should not miss him, but I do miss him, his mischief, his joyous playfulness like a young goat. He chose rightly. He was at home in the world.

I was not. Though I could not stay in the Order that my father had taught me, neither was the world for me. The world made me sick.

Not with hate. Not sick with hate. Just sick. It was wildness, churning chaos. It upset my soul, making me dizzy like a little boy spinning circles in the field. The spinning is fun at first, but then you cannot stop, because if you stop, you fall and your stomach turns inside out.

I haven't ever liked that. And I like spirit sickness least of all.

She stirs now. A little cry. O Lord. Now more. I must stop.

September 4

Mike came by today with an order. We have not had an order in a while, because the English are struggling, so Mike says. So this is good. He is a funny one, Mike is, so talkative. Big and loud. So large, his truck barely holds him.

I do not ask him any questions, not about the world, but he always talks to me about the world anyway. I try not to listen, but Gracious Lord, does that man talk. He is so angry about the president and the government and the Congress, and he uses words he knows I would rather not hear.

I think he forgets, or he says it because he knows he can and I will forgive him. I can't say.

But the order is a big one, bigger than I had hoped. I will need help with it. So many pieces! I remember how large the houses were, the houses of the very rich. Funny, that the very rich want such simple, handcrafted things. So much, for one house. But Mike says it is just one order, from one person.

There will be much work. My hands are eager for it.

Isaak visited in the late afternoon, before dinner. We sat and shared some lemonade, and talked about what he thinks he will preach on this Sunday. He likes to talk to others before he speaks, to hear what they have to say. He is a good friend.

September 5

I am very tired tonight. Today was very busy, and my hands and back are tired. Four chairs, perfect and complete, rest in the shop. This is good. It was a good day, even though I am tired.

I also walked the farm today, all of it, all the way around. I do this, just to see how things are. I could ride Nettie, and that would be quicker, but I choose not to. It lets me stop, to see things that I would otherwise miss, to feel the grass against my pant legs. We have forty-eight acres, about all we can manage, being such a small family. Five or six we rotate in and out of use for planting, there are a few patches of trees for windbreaks, and a stand of trees on about two acres to the northern corner of the property. That is good for firewood. The rest we have as pasture for our small herd of cattle. Thirty-five head, some for milking, but most for beef. It is not a long circuit, although the day was hot. And from what I see, things are well. The fields look fine, ready for the plowing and planting for the fall.

I worry about the fields. Not this year or the next, not now when we are still strong. But it will be hard as Hannah and I grow older. Around us, our friends are a help, but it is odd to have so little family around us. No sisters or brothers, no cousins. It was a hard choice to come here.

But my father's settlement? The settlement of my uncle and all of my family? Though my blood was there, my spirit could not stay there. It could not, not if my soul was to survive. Hannah, too. It was so much worse for her. Even now, I can feel the memories of it pressing on me.

And now I am awake, and it is late.

Hannah tells me that I must sleep, that the care of Sadie is for her to do as my helpmate, and I tell her that she is right, and that I am a fool. But still, I am her husband, and when I say my heart is moved for our sweet, strange little bird, that I am her father and my strength must be hers, she cannot say no. I see the tiredness in her eyes, too.

I tell her that we are two together, made stronger just as Solomon said in his wisdom, and that Sadie is no burden but is a blessing to test and strengthen us, and other things I remember from worship.

"You *are* a fool," she says, and those words were never spoken with such love.

My prayers are all about Sadie, in the morning and the evening. I should be better about praying for others, but I cannot think of much but her. I read back across these pages, and it has been nearly a year now since it began.

I did not understand, not at first, the strangeness that

overcame her that morning. She woke, but did not dress, and did not do as she was asked. Hannah came to me, and at first we together were stern.

She had always been so bright, so light. But now that brightness burned, and the lightness was brittle. Nothing made sense, nothing she said, and her hands danced like fires as she jabbered and moved about the house.

I chastised her at first. What did I know, O Lord? Sometimes anger rises up, as it did with my father. I am not so different, as much as I try to be. So the words came out.

"Do not be lazy! Do not speak such idle talk! Listen to me!"

But my words were unheard, and when I realized her eyes did not see me, my fatherly anger melted to fear.

And then she fell hard on the hard wood floor, and her body drew up like a bow, and her eyes rolled back, and she was choking on her tongue.

It was a terrible sound, like blood in the throat of a slaughtering pig. I remember it so well I can hear it.

I can still hear it.

September 6

Jacob was a great help today. His hands are still so young, but he strengthens. He is growing, up to my shoulders now. More important, his mind is sharp. He takes to the craft so swiftly, so easily. The chest of drawers for Mike will be done, and even sooner and better than if only my own hands had done it. Only five more pieces. A blessing, indeed, is a son who honors his father with the labor of his hands.

Hannah tells me it was not so good with Sadie today, not good at all. She did not sleep last night, that I know. And she was so distressed today, Hannah says. There were no seizures, but she is so unhappy.

She broods, and will only sleep, or talk in strange circles, as she has since it got worse.

But now it is only one thing she can seem to think about. She talks about the lights, and about the darkness. The skies are bright with angel wings, she will shout, suddenly. The English fall! The English fall! Again and again she says this. The skies filled with angel wings, about the English, and about the fall. We give her the medicine, and it quiets her, but the quiet passes more quickly.

I confess I am troubled, and I am praying much over it.

Sadie was always different. Before the doctors told us there was something wrong, before the seizures, she was different. She was born with a caul, which means nothing. I have seen calves born with cauls, and there is no magic I can see in them. They get eaten, just like all of the other calves. Their jerky tastes no different from regular jerky. But sometimes the old women still talk, Hannah tells me.

The angel's touch, some said she had. And the folk still remember what she said about Bishop Beiler, before even the first signs of the cancer. And about the Hostetler girl. And about that calf. It was strange, and Bishop Schrock had many talks with me about the whisperings that should not be part of the Order.

"There is no Christ in this," he said. "This seems the Devil's work," he said.

I nodded, but told him she was a good girl, because she was, even if she did say strange things. I felt anger, too, for Bishop Schrock can be a hard man. Of the bishops in this district, his heart turns most quickly to discipline. But prayer and more prayer returned my heart to the grace of Christ.

And now she moans in the night, and I hear her whisper. Every night, every night for a month, as I read back.

And every night, it is the same thing.

The angel wings, and the sky, and the English. And the fall.

Though she is my little girl, barely more than a child, the hairs rise on my arms as I write this. It is just a sickness, I say to my soul. Just a sickness of the mind.

But I do not believe myself when I say it. I cannot but worry that something bad will happen.

September 7

Worship was good today, but it was very hard for Sadie. In the singing, she is fine, but the first sermon she struggles, and the main sermon is difficult for her to manage, and the long silence as we pray together is very very hard. It strains her. And as hard as it is for Sadie, it's harder for Hannah. She watches her. She worries. Even when Sadie seems calm, she worries. The medicine stilled her enough for the day, but things got worse after the sun set.

Tonight Sadie hurt Hannah, but she does not want me to tell the doctor or the deacons. Sadie's arm lashed out as she cried and shouted and flailed. She bloodied Hannah's nose and bruised her eye. She did not mean to, I know she did not. It was like she did not notice her mother was even there.

I had to hold her, and hold her, until the medicine and the strength of my arms stilled her. So thin and frail she is now. I feared bruising her, but I was afraid she would hurt herself even worse.

It was hard on Hannah, good mother that she is. I don't want them to take her away, cried Hannah. I cannot lose my baby, cried Hannah.

She remembers how David, the second of the Sorensons' children, became. So angry, so hateful. They tried to care for him, and prayed, but though he had chosen to return, his soul was broken and shattered. It was like keeping a wild dog in the house, and they had to think of their other children. Just twenty-one. Such a young man. The English call it *skitzofrenia*, I think that is the word, I am not sure.

I mean, I know that is how you say it, but I also know that I am spelling it wrong. I will look in the dictionary later.

Jacob will be our last. Just Jacob and Sadie, both blessings in their own ways.

Sarah died inside Hannah, and it was then the Lord's desire to close her womb. We don't want to lose Sadie, our first, to have her leave the house to be treated among the English. We lost Sarah. We lost the promise of a full house, of children to work by our side, to be our strength when age takes us. This would be a third loss. With God's help we would bear it, but it would be hard.

We prayed together, and with Jacob, that the Lord might bring Sadie healing. We say these prayers often. I know God hears them. The time will come. We have to be patient.

I will see what the doctor can do tomorrow. I will be true, but gentle with truth.

I am very tired.

September 9

Awoke before the sun, even before cockcrow. My mind leaps to all that must be done.

The cows gave a little less milk today. The steers I bought to fatten up for the winter are coming along well, putting on plenty of weight and eating well.

Plowed three acres and put in the wheat. That was my day. Jacob watered the horses, good lad.

TONIGHT SHE IS QUIET. The new medicine helps, thanks be to God. The doctor came, Doctor Jones, and though we did not tell him everything, I know he knew that things were harder. We held him in prayer. He is a Baptist, he says. A good man. He has always had kindness in his heart.

I am tired, but I'm still awake, and so I stood outside for a while. It was beautiful, the stars bright. But brighter still was the glow of Lancaster, off to the south, so many miles away. It is not really dark at night. I notice this. I wonder about my grandfather's father, and how he and I share the same place, yet even as we live beyond the English and their ways, their light still fills our skies.

I think of Mike, and his anger. Today he came to check on the order, and when he talked, he was very angry about something he had heard on the radio in his truck. The radio person was angry about "the global warming hoax," and "the economy," and everything. I do not know why Mike listens to the radio if all he receives is anger, but he does. The things I hear in my life are so different. I read. I listen to the worship, and to the singing, and to the teachings, and that is not what I receive. I listen to the stillness in our times of silent prayer especially.

It is a funny thing, to listen to silence. I do it when I am done with my prayers for my neighbors and my own struggling soul and the world around me. Then, I try not to pray at all. Why would God need to hear me babbling on about myself? Instead, I try to listen.

Even in silent prayer, when we are in worship, all is not quiet. Not if you are really listening. All around me, my brothers and sisters move and shift and rustle, like young leaves in a soft spring breeze. It is calming, to hear them. And a comfort.

I wish, sometimes, that Mike could hear such things.

But I am not Mike.

Mike was mad again at the president, and about the Congress. Apparently things are bad among the English. Another bridge failed last week, and many died. The lights in Lancaster have been dark more often lately. Others in this district do not see it. Best to sleep early after a long day, if you can. But I am often awake at night. The stars are so much easier to see, when the lights are out.

Mike is angry about that too. He says it's all a mess, that no one trusts anyone, that nothing seems to work. But mostly, he talks about how he is no longer free, and how the new taxes make it hard to buy fuel to drive his big truck.

I don't know. This has been a strange year again, sometimes so hot, at other times too cool. The rain has not come often these past few years, and when it comes, it comes fierce like a fever. Deacon Sorenson remembers when it wasn't so, and will fret now and again, although we know that we must take what the Lord gives us.

Many have lost their crops, and we have had to help many families. There has been much praying, but little has changed. Perhaps this is the work of the English. Others do not say it, but I do think it. I think it often. If they can fill the night sky with wasted light, perhaps this heat is theirs as well.

But it is all right. I am not English. I would never wish to be.

AND YET, AND YET. I say I am not English, and still I write this. I write it in English. These words, this way, these thoughts. Not *Deitsch*. Not the language I was taught as a boy, not the language of our songs and the Ordnung. The Order. I can barely even think in that language now, not as my mind works.

I can speak *Deitsch*, yes, of course. I speak it almost every day. I have not forgotten the language of our community, or of my father. But it is not the language I hear when I dream. It is not the language of my soul. My father would remind me of that, as I would fall into speaking it. It was another reason to be ashamed.

My mind, which is now filled with silly, silly thoughts. Childish thoughts. Dwelling on things, chewing over them like a cow with its cud.

I must sleep.

September 10

I rose with Hannah and Jacob. Milked the cows, then set out feed for the rest of the cattle, and fed and watered the horses, while Jacob collected eggs. One of the hens has not laid for several weeks. I think I must slaughter it. It is a shame, she is not old, but there are two dozen others. So we will have chicken.

It is so hot today. It has been difficult to work, and Hannah has been careful in the kitchen. But we do what we can, as we can.

I feel so thankful, for the blessings of God and the goodness of His Providence. Sadie is quiet and more at peace, and today when I came in for dinner, she smiled at me as she had as a little girl. I have said a special prayer for the doctor, and his kindness.

I was reminded, in a flash of remembering, of a time when she was a girl. It was a particular moment. I do not know why I remember it. It was after the harvest, just a few years ago, and we had walked to the edge of a field, then down a hillside.

Eleven she was, I think.

We sat together, father and daughter, quiet but for the apples she had brought for us, which we ate. Down the hillside was a road, a great serpent of highway, on which passed many cars. We watched them, she and I, for a while.

And then she asked about the cars, and the people.

"There are so many, Dadi," she said. "Are there little girls like me in the cars?" I said yes. "What are they like?" I said they are English. They are the world. They are so busy, they have no time to see God or each other.

She looked sad. "I think God loves them," she said. "Even if they don't know it."

I agreed. God loves all of his children, I said. But we must learn how to love him back.

She got up.

"It makes me so sad," she said. And then she walked up the hill, her skirt brushing across the long grass.

Such a kind-hearted girl, my gentle, strange Sadie was. Is. She must still be, under the cries and the darkness. I say a prayer, that her kindness is not broken, too. The window is open, and outside it smells like rain. And the horizon is alight with lightning.

September 11

Today there was much work, but not on the furniture or in the fields.

The storms came deep in the night last night, scouring. Terrible storms, as bad as the spring. The winds beat the house like fists. Tonight as I write, the lights in the city are still out, and the sky is dark, but among us, that means nothing. But there was so much broken, so much. Shingles down. A barn damaged. The Fishers got the worst of it, had to shelter in their cellar.

Jacob came with me out to the Fishers' farm. So many trees fallen. So much broken, like a great hand had swept across the land. It was a very familiar scene.

Is it right for me to be proud of Jacob? I feel pride in my heart for the strength of this boy, almost a man, and how eager his heart was to labor by my side.

He and I and all of us worked for much of the day, because so much was broken. That old oak had rested the Fisher home in shade for a hundred years, and still it was shattered, one large branch crashed through the roof, the trunk falling away by God's grace. Some of the men gathered with bucksaws, others with two-man saws. We worked together, and that great old trunk came apart, piece by piece.

It was such an old thing, that oak, but still so very alive. There was no rot in it. It was a healthy, strong, living tree. And yet it was time for it to die. By midwinter, perhaps, the wood will be cured enough for firewood.

Jacob and I, once we'd pulled that tree from the roof, joined the Stolfutzes in replacing the damaged soffits and joists. I had brought wood, and others had brought new sub-roofing and shingles. So many hands at work, Isaak and his sons, now almost men. Joseph and his boys, so diligent in their youth.

It was hard work, and the storms had not brought cool with them, but more heat. We drank the water, and took breaks in the shade, and we sweated. Jacob worked as hard as any of us, and I had to remind him sometimes to stop and come out of the sun. He has such a precise hand, and attends to the work before him.

By late afternoon, the roof was repaired, and we returned home.

Sadie was calm today. It was a good day for her. She spoke evenly, and did not seem angry, and had helped Hannah with preparation for the dinner. Truly, the Lord does answer our prayers. We must just be patient.

September 12

It is so hot. It gets so hot. More rain again today, not fierce, but the heat hangs in the wet air.

Mike stopped by again today, to check in on the order. The client is impatient, he says, although it has only been a week. The client was angry because he couldn't reach Mike yesterday, and only got through on his cell phone this morning. But there was no power in the town, so nothing was working. He could not get gas, and there were lines, and people were not getting along. Mike is angry, because he is tired and has not slept well. The power comes on and off, and his house does not cool with air-conditioned air, because the compressor blew.

Mike wishes the client would understand that things take time and are more difficult. The client should know this. Mike was hot and angry, and was not sympathetic, and said so in his profane way.

He knows this will take time, but it is hard for the client to understand. I wish I could talk with them, but they are far away, near Washington, DC, and do not wish to come here. Mike told them they could, but they do not want to, because they are too busy.

Mike says the impatience is because of the internet, because everyone now wants everything the moment they want it. I remember this from when I was jumping around in the world. I remember how people would walk around not even seeing each other, eyes down into their rectangles of light. No one was where they were.

So busy, the English are, and there was so much in my time there that was terrible. I was at a party those years ago when I went running around, I remember, with a friend, and one of his friends asked to show me something, and I said sure, and we sat at the computer and he showed me. It took me a moment, and then I had to look away. It was pornography, something strange, something even most English found horrible, and they laughed as I recoiled. They knew it would horrify me. It was funny for them, I think. It was not as things ever would or could be with Hannah.

And yet this is how the English live now. Whatever they want is there, even their most terrible darkness. So different from when the Order stepped away. There was a time when we were almost alike. All rode on horseback. Oil lit all homes, be they English or of the Order. We all worked the land. But now?

Now the English have their wild magics, so different it becomes hard to understand.

Such a wild terrible mess, the world is now. I am glad that I am not in it.

I WRITE AGAIN TONIGHT, because I cannot sleep. It is so hot, the blasting sun of day hanging in the wet air. We can none of us sleep, except for Sadie, who has taken her medicine. Hannah and Jacob moved out to the root cellar, and set down one of our mattresses in the cool of the earth. I carried Sadie, who nestled light in my arms, half asleep. They rest down there, all three of them. It is cooler there, resting in the earth.

But I cannot sleep. So here on the porch I look out at the night, and wish that the air was not so still.

Sometimes when I cannot sleep, I read. So I will read the *Martyrs Mirror*, and reflect on those who gave their lives for what we believe.

I will sleep, soon.

September 14

I did not write yesterday. And the Sabbath worship was good today. We gathered at the Sorensons', and the room was filled with the old songs and the honest smell of sweat as we sat in silent prayer. Deacon Sorenson preached the first and the second sermons. They were good and simple. He was a good choice for preacher, and he mixes the duties of deacon and preacher with grace.

· I know all men are to preach if they are chosen, and that it is not to ever be a source of pride or arrogance. But just as some men are better in the fields and others better with tools, some speak better than others.

With all gathered in together, it became very hot. It was easy to forget in the preaching and in the singing, but as we sat in silent prayer, the heat was all around us. After a time old Mrs. Miller collapsed and had to be cooled down with water. But the women took care of that.

Perhaps the greatest blessing was that Sadie was calm again, and she even sang. Just a little bit, but I could hear her. It made Hannah smile. I was glad.

But then I was also ashamed, ashamed about this very thing I do now.

I am wondering about this writing.

I see back six months, and I was wondering then. For so many years, I was sure that it was prideful, my secret sin, my shame. As a boy, I was convicted of that from the sermons of my uncle. Today, Deacon Sorenson's preaching was simple and good, but though he did not mean to do so, he stirred an old hurt in me. Much like a cold, wet day does not mean to make that long broken bone ache. It was not his fault.

Deacon Sorenson preached about secrets and shame, and about how nothing can be hidden from God. He taught about how hiding thoughts keeps us from being together, and staying true to the Order, and to Christ. None of that is wrong, I think. Much of what he had to say was right and true.

There is shame that we feel that is a good shame. It comes as we see how we hurt others and ignore God. But there is a bad shame that is used to hurt others and turn them away from God. I used to be told that this act, this act I am doing right now in writing and remembering, worse yet in English, was just such a shameful thing.

It was what I was told, back when I was a boy. I was told it so much that part of me still wants to be ashamed. That teaching cut a deep furrow in me. Like all people, I cling to my past, and even to the pain of my past. It is who I am. It seems hard to believe, here in this place.

Writing about crops served a purpose, my uncle would say. About yourself? It is selfishness. It was why he and others left their homes, and formed their own community. Others were not as holy. Others had abandoned the one right path, the real Ordnung.

I can hear the prayer my uncle would have me be praying. "Lord, keep me from this," I would say. "Silence my desire. Make me your servant. Guide me to your will. This will be the last of these entries. I will cast this away. In Jesus' name, Amen." I can hear it. But I cannot pray it. I will not pray it.

I know that in this place, I will not be asked to pray it. That is why we came here, to this place, to this district, to this old settlement.

And I will be allowed to remember. I am grateful for that here. And grateful for Preacher Sorenson, for the day of contemplation.

AFTER OUR EVENING PRAYERS, Sadie came over to me, and whispered in my ear.

"It is all right to remember, Dadi. It is important." I was startled, and pulled back. "God says so," she said, smiling.

Then she went to get ready for bed. She did not say another thing.

Funny, how she knows. And again, I shiver, as if suddenly cold, at what that might mean.

September 15

Today was again hot, the sky a dull, cloudless blue, the sun set in it bright and fierce and terrible. Jacob and I worked awhile in the morning, and we were able to make some progress. But the going was slow, and by noon the workshop was an oven.

Sadie was able to work with Hannah in the kitchen this morning, canning preserves and making apple butter. She seemed a little better.

The oats are coming in, not the best, but coming in.

I went across to the Fishers, who were offering up wood from their fallen oak. I took a tenth of a cord, no more, for wood has been easy to come by. Joseph asked if they could come visiting tomorrow, and I said sure.

Nettie and Pearl were so hot when we returned, mouths all foam and eyes a little wild. I watered and splashed them with buckets of cool well water.

Together we worked in the orchard in the early evening, gathering in five bushels of apples. Our trees have taken some damage from the storms, and the apples are smaller and less plentiful this year. But the damage is not too much, and the water in the well still holds, and we are not in need. The Lord is gracious with his harvest, still, and it is enough for our family and our simple needs.

Although we would be blessed with a cooling rain.

September 16

The rain did not come, but the winds blew, and the day is cooler.

This early morning, after the milking, Jacob and I slaughtered a pig, the big one. Much of the morning was cutting and preparing, and setting the meat into the freezer.

There will be more, but it was the whole work of our morning. It took longer than anticipated, and our breakfast was no longer warm, but Hannah was forgiving, even as she chided us.

After breakfast, we finished building the last of the order. Mike will be pleased. I sent Jacob to the community phone, so that we could tell Mike.

Hannah prepared simple food, slaw and some meat pies, and Sadie helped, as the Fishers were to come in the late afternoon. Joseph and Rachel and their five, plus Rachel pregnant again, they have been blessed and fruitful. And they are still not old. There will be more children, a larger family.

Their oldest, also Rachel, is fourteen just like our Sadie, then Fritz and Hosheah, then Mariam, then Micah.

It was a lively afternoon. The Fishers came in their wagon and a buggy, and Jacob was at once off with the boys to play. Sadie was calm, and she and Rachel went to talking and walking for a while, as Hannah and the older Rachel rested with lemonade before cooking for the evening.

Joseph and I sat, and we talked. He was worried about the Johansons, who operate the 375 acres just to the south of his own. They had always had problems, and always been the sort of family that struggles, even in the good times when the harvest was good and the money was plentiful. Even the best blessings of Providence cannot turn a soul from sorrow if it has set itself down that path.

But with the terrible weather, and the power outages, and the trouble, they were suffering. The hot and dry summer stunted their corn, and all they grew was corn. When the fierce rains began again, their fields were much damaged. Some rains, they can handle, but two or three inches an hour?

Joseph shook his head as he spoke. The Johansons had seen almost no yield this year. The herbicide-treated soil had no quackgrass, nothing to hold it, and the slight incline of much of that property meant that much corn and soil were washed away. I had seen it, the washes cutting across what had been good earth.

The Johansons also had several chicken coops, long flat structures with hens by the tens of thousands, all packed into crates. That had been a good cash yield, from one of the big companies that puts chicken into the stores in the cities. But then the power failed midsummer, not one of the storm outages, but when one power company wouldn't provide to another. The fans failed, and the coops became ovens. Most of the hens died.

Mr. Johanson was beside himself, deep in debt to the bank, and the loans and loan guarantees and payments from the government that used to tide English farmers over no longer came through. Something about China, and austerity measures. Mike has told me about these things, too.

Joseph was worried, because his neighbor had taken to drinking more and more. Two nights before, there had been angry shouting in the distance. It was just drunkenness and rage, as he stumbled through the fields shouting with a bottle in his hand, cursing uselessly at his own fields, blasting the sun-blasted earth with his hate. The police came, called by another neighbor. Very sad thing, we both thought.

So we prayed together for his neighbor, for the family. And then we ate, and gave thanks. It was good, to be together. A blessing.

I WAS LOOKING OUT across our little farm, in the half-darkness of the night, and giving thanks for the blessing we had been given, when she was suddenly by my side without my knowing it. Like a wraith, she moves sometimes, my Sadie.

I asked her how she had enjoyed her time with Rachel, and she smiled and said it was good to see her.

She looked at the night sky, dimming at the cool of day. She said that the angels were coming soon. The sky will be filled with their wings. She was not upset, as she had been before. There was no seizure. She was very calm. But she was still saying it.

"We will be all right, when they come," she said. "But it will not be easy, Dadi."

And then she went inside. "It's late, Dadi," she called to me. "Come in."

September 18

For the first time in a month, a gentle morning rain, soft and long and soaking. It will do the wheat good.

Mike came in his truck today, with the trailer. He was in a good mood. The buyer had transferred money, right on schedule, into Mike's bank account. It is electronic, the payment, but Mike deals with that part of the business. What matters is that the payment was made. Mike had taken his broker's fee, plus the costs for transporting the goods based on distance, fair as we had always agreed.

He brought cash with him, a large fat envelope, which he counted out once and again for me. I always tell him that I trust him, but he always laughs and says it is good to be sure.

When business was done, we talked. Or rather, he talked. I mostly listen. He talked about what was in the news, more about the cutbacks, about discontent in the military because of benefit reductions, and some large demonstration that got angry in Washington. But he seemed less worried, because, for this week, his portion of the furniture sale would help with his bills. It was good to see him so relaxed. It is so rare.

He always worries. His life is so difficult, so chaotic. He tells me of his struggles with his ex-wife, of custody issues and how unhappy his two children are, of his girlfriend who is pregnant, and how things are with the two of them.

Things with them are not good.

It isn't easy, and never seems to get easier. For the years I have known him, it is always the same. Patterns of sadness and anger passing through his life like the seasons of harvest and planting.

Where we have the Sabbath, and the apples, and the oats, and the wheat, and the corn, he has the fights, and the anger from his radio, and the anger of his sons, and the bitterness of his broken life with Shauna. I think that is his ex-wife's name, although usually there is a profanity before he says it. He says it that way so much that sometimes I wonder if that is her actual name.

And then the words came to me: The sorrows are planted, and they grow strong in the earth of his life, and they rise up, and there is harvest.

I think that, but I would not speak it to him. He does not need me to tell him something he knows already.

He does not need me to tell him anything, I think. He needs me to listen. So I do.

In so many ways, he is a good man, for all of his bluster and anger and cynicism. Yet contentment seems out of his reach.

But today, he was happy. If just for a moment.

IN THE HOUR AFTER dinner, as the night was gently
cool, I sat with Hannah awhile. The table was cleared and
the horses stabled, and evening prayers were said. Jacob was
asleep, and Sadie was calm. We sat, and we did not talk much.

It was a good thing, to sit, calm and quiet.

Then she asked, "Jay?" And I said, yes? "Does Sadie seem
better, Jay?" I said I did not know, but that she seemed hap-
pier. I said it because it was true.

"Will she be able to stay with us?" I said yes, because I
knew we would be able to make do, although in my heart I
knew that when age came upon us, she would have to stay
with our son.

She was silent for a moment. "What of a husband? How
can she marry? How . . ." And I hushed her, and said I was
not sure, but that I worried about it, too. She is still only
fourteen, I reminded. And she is better lately.

This sounded empty in my ears as I said it, but I said it
anyway.

"Then why does she still talk as she does," asked Hannah.
"The women talk about it, and it troubles the deacons. Always
the same these last months, always about the angels and the
English. Terrible, strange things." I said that I did not know,
but yes, it was always the same.

"You know about the things she says," whispered Hannah.
Her eyes turned up, brown and anxious. My Hannah, she is
never anxious. "Do you think it is true?" she asked. "It frightens me, sometimes." There was a catch in her voice, and she
pressed against my arm. I held her closer.

I did not know what to say, and so I said that such things were not mine to know.

We sat for a little while after that, and then she went up to prepare for bed.

I sat for a while, and wrote this, but I know tomorrow will be a long day.

September 19

I rose as I always do, just before the sun rises. But in the barn this morning was Sadie, already up, dressed . . . if a little messily . . . and milking. Just as she had before. Jacob was gathering eggs.

Sadie smiled at me, looking up for a moment, and said, "Good morning, Dadi," and went back to her milking.

I said good morning back. I do not know why I felt sadness, but for a moment, I did. But by the time I was walking to hitch the horses to the plow to prepare two more acres for the wheat, I was no longer sorrowful.

And the air was cooler, the first truly cool day for many, many months.

IN THE AFTERNOON, BISHOP and Mrs. Schrock came for an unexpected visit. Mrs. Schrock talked with Hannah, maybe about Sadie. This would be good for Hannah, because Mrs. Schrock is frail, but a gentle, quiet heart, and very good at prayer.

Bishop Schrock talked with me, and it was about Mike. He was concerned for my soul, being around such a one. He was thinking that I should consider ending our partnership, of finding another to seek the orders for my woodshop among the English.

"There are English and there are English," he said. "He is a divorced man," he said, "and a drunkard. In the town I heard that the police had to be called because of their fighting. He is not someone you should be associating with. He might steal from you, and might bring shame on all of us."

Bishop Schrock talked for quite a while. When he preaches, this is also true.

I listened, mostly. We have had this conversation before. Back in August, on the 10th. And, let me look back. Yes, July 14th. And other times. Bishop Schrock is a persistent man, so different from Bishop Beiler.

And I answered that I was very sorry that Mike was having such a hard time, and that such things were common now among the English. And I said, as I have every time we have spoken of this, that though the English cannot be of the Order, and we cannot take their ways into our hearts, we must always be compassionate to them.

If I only pray for him, and do not help him through my listening and our work, then am I doing as Jesus would have me do? I said this, as I always say this. And Bishop Schrock always looks away, and his face looks as if he has hurt a tooth, his jaw working a little bit. That is how his face looks, when I say that.

Last year, when he brought his concerns about Mike to

the deacons, and they talked, that is what I said. I said other things, too, but that was the heart of it. And they decided what they decided. That is why I still work with Mike.

"I will pray for you on this matter," said Bishop Schrock. I thanked him, and told him that I always appreciated a heart-felt prayer.

And then we talked about chickens.

September 20

The day began, and the cool was in the air as the sun rose. Fall is so close now. Sadie is helping more. Jacob was milking this morning, but she was near the house, moving methodically through the last of the everbearing strawberries, filling a small basket with the fruit.

It is so late to be gathering them, but they keep coming. Joseph Fisher told me that last year, they still had everbearing strawberries coming in late October. Of course, the frost and that one huge early snow came, but it was still so very late.

Sadie and Hannah spent the morning working on strawberry preserves, and Jacob and I killed and plucked that hen, and two broilers we'd been fattening up.

It was a slow day, a calm day. I went to sit near the road, and chewed on a bit of straw, and watched the English roar by in their cars. Car after car, *whoosh*.

Whoosh. Whoosh. Such a hurry.

But for me, it was restful, a sabbath, though not the Sabbath.

SADIE WAS STILL OUTSIDE, though it had been dark for several hours.

I heard Hannah call for her, and Sadie replied, but I did not hear what Sadie said.

I went to the kitchen, and Hannah told me to go talk with her. What did she say? I asked. Just talk with her, Hannah asked. She was trying not to be upset.

And so I went, and I sat, and I asked her what she was doing.

She was not upset. She was not unhappy. She looked at me with her large eyes set kind and sad into that slender face, and she smiled.

"I'm waiting for the angels, Dadi. I want to see them when they come."

I asked her what that meant. But she just smiled, and shook her head. "You'll see, Dadi."

Then she asked, "Dadi, can you stay with me? Can you sit awhile?"

I said that I could. "If it takes three nights, or even seven?" she asked. I told her that I could.

"It is very soon, Dadi," she said. "Very soon. I'm glad you'll sit with me."

And so we sat, for an hour, saying little. My concern faded, as she nestled against me. After a while, she gave me a little hug, and went in to go to bed. She did not seem upset.

Hannah and I talked afterward, and I told her what Sadie had said. She asked what it meant again, and I said what I had said before.

She is not angry or afraid, I added. And she has been doing so well in the kitchen and around the house.

I know, Hannah said. And then she paused, as if to say more, but she did not.

September 21

After breakfast, today was mostly apple picking. The Fishers came to join in, and then the Sorensons, as our acre and a half of trees was ready for picking, and the four of us can only gather in so much. Deacon Sorenson brought his big wagon, and three of his sons, and the eldest's wife and her new baby.

We moved from tree to tree, in groups that mingled and changed. Jacob was a help, of course. And Sadie was very busy. She laughed, and passed a smile to the middle Fisher boy. Then she went back with Hannah and Mrs. Sorenson and Mrs. Fisher to help prepare the meal for tonight.

The baskets filled quickly, and the two wagons were soon loaded. The yield was not as much as the year before, and many of the apples were small, but it was still an abundance. After a long, slow day, twenty-two bushels, with much still left on the trees. There would be plenty for sale, and for cider, and for preserves.

Then there was talking, and lemonade, and some early cider.

For dinner, ham, and freshly baked bread, and beans in the cool of the late afternoon. Deacon Sorenson said a simple blessing, as is his way. It was a very nice day.

SADIE SAT OUT AGAIN tonight, watching the sky as the stars appeared. I sat with her, of course. We mostly talked about the day, and the picking, and when I mentioned Sam Fisher, she may have blushed a little. But it was dark.

The air was cool, and as the night grew deeper, it took on the scent and crispness of autumn.

Another night like this, and we will need a fire in the stove, I said to Sadie. "I love to just watch the fire in the fireplace," she said. "So pretty, as it dances."

I agreed.

We sat for maybe an hour, until the sky was fully dark. And then she said, "Not tonight," and gave me a little hug, and went to prepare for bed.

September 22

And on the third night, the angels came and filled the heavens.

It began in early evening, as I watched, sitting with Sadie again, just as she had asked.

It was just darking, the last colors of the sun vanishing, the first stars showing, the light of the town brightening. It had been a beautiful sunset.

And then they came. A flicker here, and a flicker there, color danced in the sky. Then sheets of it, brighter and brighter, dancing wild sheets cast across the skies, beautiful purples and blues and pinks.

The sky became full of them, dancing, waving, and pulsing. They would fade a little, and strengthen, and then grow stronger and stronger.

So beautiful. But terrible. What was this? Angels? It was not as I would have thought. So bright and silent. I do not know. I do not yet know.

Hannah came, and Jacob, and we watched together, as the wings of angels lit the skies, and the earth glowed under the warm light. Jacob laughed and pointed and jumped around at the joy of it.

Then it grew so bright that it was brighter than midnight under a full moon, bright enough to see my hand, to see the house. Angel wings dipped, radiant with color, and touched the earth. There was a feeling of strangeness in the air, I do not know what it was, but the hairs on my arm rose. From fear, perhaps, because it was strange, but also because the air seemed sharp with . . . something. I do not know. But the smell changed.

"Dadi, it's so bright, what is that smell?" asked Jacob, suddenly stilled, his voice filled with awe and alarm. Hannah pulled in close, but Sadie stood separate, looking up, rocking back and forth a little.

It went on, radiant and terrible and beautiful. We stood silent.

And then Jacob said, "Dadi, look, there are no lights in the town now," he said, "and there are no lights on the road." It was true. And he was excited and frightened, and looking everywhere and talking, and then he pointed up.

"Look at the plane," he called out, and there it was, an airplane, a big one. It was not where the planes normally fly, high and moving north or south. The silhouette was low and large. There were no lights on it, or in it, just the beautiful light dancing on and behind it.

It was sideways. It was coming down.

I could see both wings, bent back dark like a broken cross, and it was floating downward, downward, very slow. It was very wrong. I began to pray.

The plane moved down, southward, like a dark, windblown leaf against the color-splashed sky. We lost it to view behind the trees.

And then there was a faint flash, and a few seconds later, a crump like a short peal of thunder.

"Oh blessed Jesus, all those people," said Hannah, and she began to pray softly and in earnest, her whispered prayers melding with mine.

Still, the skies danced, so bright, so silent.

And a few seconds later, another flash, to the north. And a minute later, another to the southwest.

Sadie turned to us, and her eyes were huge and wet with tears.

"The English fall," she said.

And then she went inside, away from the light that filled the sky over the darkened earth.

September 23

I awoke this morning, and it felt like any other morning.

We woke together, and prayed in earnest for the souls of those on the fallen plane. Such a terrible thing to see. For half of an hour, we prayed. But then the day's work called.

The air was crisp, this second day of autumn. I went out to the barn, and there was Sadie, milking. I fed the horses, then went to tend to some business in the workshop.

In the distance, there was fire, smoke rising from something big burning off to the south. Where the plane went down. It is strange that it is still burning, but the woods have been dry.

YOUNG JIM STOLFUTZ ARRIVED while the morning was still new, riding that three-year-old mare of theirs, no buggy, riding fast, faster than he should. I saw him through the window of the workshop, set down my tools, and walked out to greet him. He rode over to me, leapt off, and came up breathless, face red with excitement and the bite of the breeze. The mare was breathing hard.

"There has been something strange," he told me. "Something has happened." I told him that yes, I knew, the lights in the sky and that plane. It was a tragedy. But he shook his head, and cleared his throat.

"Dadi told me to ride, to tell you and everyone. Our neighbors the Wilsons, they say that they have no power. And Mr. Wilson's generator won't start, and their trucks won't start, and their car won't start. The radio, it doesn't work, and their cell phones don't work. Some of them turn on. But nobody hears anything.

"And our generator is dead, too, when my mami tried to use it for the washing this morning."

"Does he hear from anyone else?" I asked.

"No," said Jim. "No word from nobody. Man from Lancaster was supposed to talk with my dad, but he never showed. I just came from Mr. Fisher," he said. "He tells me that his neighbor's wife came by, scared and on foot, saying that her husband was hurt bad. Not sure why or how. But they couldn't call for help. Couldn't call an ambulance. Car won't start. Truck wouldn't start. Van wouldn't start. Mr. Fisher was with her, just about to ride over to see if he could help, maybe take them into town."

"Does anyone know anything more?" I asked.

"No sir," he said. "But there are almost no cars on the road. Pretty much nobody. The roads are so quiet, it's like everything has come to a stop. Almost the only folks moving are plain folk. Just buggies. Only seen two trucks and two cars. Strangest thing."

That was strange.

"Gotta go," shouted Jim, and he leapt up onto the mare and rode off in the direction of the Sorensons'. Again he was riding faster than he should, but he was excited. I'm not so old that I've forgotten what it was to be excited.

I went and talked to Hannah, told her I was going to go over to the Sorensons', and that I'd be back by lunch.

BEFORE I WENT, I went behind the house, to where we keep our small store of fuel and the little Honda generator that Hannah uses to power the washer. That is all we use it for. Even that would not have been permitted in my father's house, but here, few see the spiritual need for washing by hand. Perhaps it is that they actually listen to their wives here. It is simple enough to be independent, or so Bishop Beiler used to say. I turned the key. Nothing. I pulled the cord to start it. Nothing.

Hannah will not be pleased to hear this.

I WAS NOT THE only one at the Sorensons'. Jim was still there when I arrived, and his father, and the oldest Fisher boy. Deacon Sorenson and Isaak Stolfutz were talking in earnest, the younger folk listening intently.

The word was the same from every family. The English neighbors, none of them had power. Most were farm folk, and most had generators and emergency power and solar and wind turbines for when the power went out.

Almost none of it was working. Some was. But most was

not. Among the plain folk, the Michaelsons, who had permission from the deacons and Bishop Schrock to put in a solar array last year, reported it was useless, shorted out completely.

The oldest Fisher boy told what he'd learned from his dadi, who'd gone to see the Johansons. Mr. Johanson was hurt bad, been working with some power equipment in their barn, got a bad shock. Burned his hand, knocked him clean across the room, or so the Fisher boy said.

They'd bandaged it, and put on salve, and then Joseph took him in the buggy and rode to Doctor Michaels's house.

And from none of them came any word of the outside.

I asked Deacon Sorenson what he thought had happened. He thought for a moment, then another moment more.

"I suppose your Sadie knows," he said, and he smiled, faintly. "But I do not." The smile lingered on his face, an echo, meaningless.

THE REST OF THE day was spent in the workshop. Not much was new to learn, although the young men rode about quickly on their horses, telling what could be told. The fire still burned to the south, smoke still rising far off in a tall, faint column. By late afternoon, another fire was burning, a little closer, to the south–southwest.

Dinner was early, a good meal. We talked about what we had seen, and we prayed. What else was there for us to do?

As night fell, it fell darker and darker. The lights in the farms of the plain folk could be seen, but the roads were almost empty, and the skies were empty, and the glow from

Lancaster in the south was gone. In the direction of the city, here and there, a point of light, and in many other places, what seemed like distant candlelight. The same to the west, to Ephrata, and even the faint lights of Lititz to the east were out. It was dark. So very dark. The light of the English no longer filled the skies.

There, in the deep black ink, were only stars. I watched for a while, because the skies were so different. Every constellation stood bright. Stars I had not seen, cannot remember seeing, were there and bright. The Milky Way was clear and visible. Amazing.

Up high, a plane, just one, lights blinking, was flying very very high and very fast. It was the first I'd seen. It moved southward, and I watched until it passed to the far horizon.

Then, with the cool coming, I came in to bed.

September 24

The morning was as it always was, except in the south that fire still burned. It is a little warmer again today but still feels like autumn. After the morning in the field, I went to my shop, and there Jacob and I worked for a while. But there was no word from Mike.

Joseph Fisher came by midmorning, and we talked. He had gone to his neighbor's home the day before, and then taken the ride to town, taken Mr. Johanson to Dr. Michaels to have his hand looked at. The burn was very bad, and they were afraid of infection, and he had no feeling in his hand.

The roads were empty, except for plain folk and some on bicycles. So many cars were abandoned, some just left by the roadside, many just in the middle of the road.

Dr. Michaels was at home, and he was able to treat Mr. Johanson, rebandaging his hand and providing some antibiotics. He was usually at the community hospital in Ephrata on Thursdays, but as he told Joseph, nothing at the hospital was working. None of his equipment. None of the machines.

The generators that provided them with emergency electricity did not work, and the ambulances did not work. Though Dr. Michaels could not start his truck to drive to town, he had ridden his bicycle those miles to the east in the morning. And then he had ridden back.

Everything in town was a mess, and nothing was working, but Dr. Michaels did not say much more than that, and Joseph did not ask. Dr. Michaels did not know much. He returned with Mr. Johanson to his home, with medicine for the burn and for the pain.

Joseph thought it was all very strange and terrible, and he asked about the lights in the sky and what they might have meant. "I have never seen their like," he said. "What did you think of them?"

I did not share what Sadie had been saying, as I knew that tales move from ear to ear even among the plain folk.

I told him that God would provide for his people, but that I also knew that sometimes there were times of terrible hardship. I said I did not know exactly what it meant.

"Do you think they were angels?" he asked, and his earnest look was very clear. He had heard the talk.

I told him no, that I did not. They were something, I said. And all things are from God. But I did not think they were angels. They had the beauty of angels, I said. But they were more like the sunrise. Or a storm. They were not living as angels live.

I said there was a word for it, but that I couldn't remember it. But I knew it was something I had seen.

"Yes, I think so, too," he said. "Like a storm, whatever that was."

We sat and talked for a while longer, and then he returned home.

IT IS LATE AGAIN, and I am awake, and the sky is dark. All sleep, but I do not. The night is not as cool as I thought it might be, as if summer pushes to return.

In the far distance, there is a light near Lancaster. But it is the light of a large fire, fierce and flickering. I watch for a while, as I write this.

September 25

Busy morning, it has been.

The morning filled with the gift of work, as always, and we prepared to go to the Michaelsons' to help harvest, Jacob and I. We will go soon. Hannah busied herself with the remainder of the apples from our harvest, and with canning the beans and the peas that Sadie and Jacob harvested in the cool of the morning after milking and feeding was done.

Sadie seems so calm now, so at ease within herself. Quieter, perhaps. But not unhappy, and strangely focused. But I was distracted. I cannot help but look to the south. The smoke rises now from several places. It has not stopped.

And the skies are still quiet. This morning another airplane flew by and then another, very small and high and fast, but those are the only ones I have seen today. Friday is always a busy day for the English in the skies, and yet the lines of cloud that crisscross the heavens are gone. Contrails, I believe they are called.

I am wondering, this Friday, about Mike. He was to come and talk with me this morning, but he did not.

I must be off. Much still to do today. But I wonder at how Mike is.

THE MICHAELSON FARM IS a bustling one, such a large family can care for much land. Eight children, all as able and capable as their parents. And today many gathered to help them prepare the oats for harvest. Jacob accompanied me, this for the first time. We and the Fishers and the Sorenson boys and the four oldest Michaelson boys. Also there were the three Schrock boys . . . men now, really . . . and both Beiler boys. We gathered behind Jon Michaelson's grain binder, and as his team drew it on, we gathered the bundles and shocked them.

As we shocked, we talked. The last few days had been harder for many of us. The Schrocks' dairy cows could not be milked except by hand, because the milking machine had failed. Neighbors are helping, but all are finding more time must be taken for everything. Less can be done. It is nothing we cannot bear.

There was much talk about how the threshing of the oats might be accomplished. There are two threshers, both old Deeres. Neither is yet working, but Young Jon Michaelson believes he can have the older one running soon. Some rewiring, something to do with shorts and failed circuits, and he was sure of it.

All talked about what they had heard from those of the

English around us. The lights were aurora, they were saying, the Northern Lights. I think now I remember seeing a picture of them in a book once, very long ago. Not angels, as angelic as they seemed.

But such lights never come so far south, never in the memory of any who live here. And they are never as bright.

It was a storm, the rumor goes, but not an earthly one. It was a storm in the heavens, a storm from the sun. And though one would not know it from here, because today has been like almost any other day among the simple folk, the English are struggling. Many are our friends, our neighbors.

And the storm did not just hit the English we know. It is not just the English around us. The news was that this was not just us, and not just Pennsylvania.

It is all of the English. Everywhere. It is the whole world.

This was enough to keep us all in silence for a while.

There was not much to know, except that everywhere, almost nothing was working. Nothing was moving. Some with working radios would pick up occasional sounds, but they learned nothing. And the satellites that carry so much of what people hear were now dead rocks in the heavens.

The cards and computers that make business possible among the English? None of them were working. None of them. It was, Willis Schrock said, a very hard thing. He'd gone to talk with some of his friends, other farmers. So few kept things on paper now. So many businesses, so many banks, and it was as if everything had been forgotten. The records and the copies of records were just gone.

"How can you even know what it is that you have? How can you even know what belongs to who?" He scratched at his beard, which made him for a moment look just like his father. "I do not even know how they will work."

And I had not been thinking it, until Abram Beiler said it. "Those who farm will struggle," he said, "but . . ."

And he paused. He was a bright man, like his father had been before he passed. "I do not know how the English will cope," he said. "How will they eat, if they cannot move their crops and food? I have seen so little moving. I have seen only two cars, and a truck. And some planes. There are stories that the army is moving, that more of their things work. But even the rails aren't working."

"There are so many in the cities. So many. You remember, Jacob," he said to me directly. "You remember what it was like."

I nodded in agreement, and he went on. "And they live as if today is the only day, and know nothing except the ways of their busyness. And now? Now what will they do? Food for today, and for tomorrow, but the winter comes."

"But perhaps they can fix the things," said Young Jon. Always hopeful, he was. "I can fix the thresher. I know I can," he said. "I can see where it is shorted out. It will be better once I get the replacement part. It has only been three days. A lot of people are more careful now, with all the storms and weather."

"That is my prayer," said Abram. "But it makes me think of my father, as the cancer spread. It was not one thing, as he died. It was everything. It was everywhere in him, and when everywhere is broken, the body cannot mend. If there is no place that has strength, then death comes quickly."

"I hope that it is not like that," said Abram. And then there was silence again.

Sometimes we sing and laugh as we work, but talk and singing and laughter felt very far away.

We worked the shocks, in the hot sun, so hot for a late September Friday, and though some hearts were heavy, we were grateful to the Lord for the gift of his creation.

When we got home, I could hear, far away, the sounds of vehicles moving, many of them, off to the west. Maybe thirty or forty vehicles, moving south.

HANNAH HAD FINISHED PREPARING our meal when we returned home, and the kitchen was hot with the rich smell of stew and vegetables. I asked after Sadie, who was not in the kitchen helping as she has been more and more of late.

"In the garden," said Hannah. "She's in the garden, talking with Liza Schrock and Rachel Fisher."

Woman talk, I was tempted to think, but I know that it was more than that. Liza is as kind as Ellis is hard, and Rachel Fisher is gifted like no other I know in the graces of prayer. My heart stirred for a moment to worry, because both have been a strength to Hannah and Sadie when Sadie's illness has taken her. They have been in our house in some very hard times.

I paused for a moment.

"Is she all right?" I asked. "Is there . . ." and words stumbled in my mouth.

But Hannah smiled, her lips pursed as they do when she is thinking many things all at once.

"No, no, she has been busy about her chores today. She seems well. They are talking and praying. There has been much talk, you know there has, in the last few days, with all of this going on."

Yes, I know, I said, because I had heard some of it, some about our Sadie, when we were out in the fields. Even among the menfolk, there was talk, although just a little. The stories about her strange brokenness have a way of being told and retold.

I know there is talk, I said.

"Well, Lizabet and Rachel just wanted to talk with her, is all," said Hannah, as she sliced up a zucchini.

Well, I said, that's good.

Hannah made a little nod, and went about her preparations, and I felt perhaps I should attend to other things.

Jacob was out feeding and grooming the horses, as was his task each evening, and so I walked to the barn to check on a board I'd seen was loose.

It was near where the women were talking, but not too near, and I looked across and saw them sitting in a tight little triangle in the grass, their dresses bundled about them like nests. Lizabet and Rachel looked intent, as Sadie was speaking softly to them both. I saw that they were hand in hand,

and though they were talking, it did seem like they may have been in prayer.

Or in and out of talk and prayer and back into talk. Time with Lizabet could be like that, I remember.

Sadie looked up, and waved, her hand a little bird fluttering. Dadi, she mouthed, and smiled, and I saw for a moment her mother's face in her.

I waved back but walked on. Best to leave them to talking, I thought.

September 26

It was a hotter morning today, and the sun rose into a reddish, bloody haze. So much smoke around, from the fires. And it has not rained, and there is no word about rain. But then there is no word about much of anything.

I was on my way to the field to see how the oats were coming when I heard him coming. It was a motorbike, old and small and loud. It racketed past, bearing a middle-aged man. I did not know him. He did not stop. He seemed very intent on something, but I do not know what.

Hannah and Sadie hitched up Nettie this morning and took the buggy, filled with washing, over to the Stolfutz house. Their generator will still start, which is good.

I surveyed the oats, and they are still weeks from shocking. They stood below my shoulder, as I brushed through them. Leaves still mostly green. I took a kernel between my fingers, and the oat milk mingled with the dirt under my nails. Still time needed yet. They went in the earth just a little later than the Michaelsons', but this acre is a little slower. Not as rich.

We will need help for the harvest, for Jacob and I could not do this alone, but it will come.

As I stood there in the field, I heard a rumbling and thundering. Not rain, but a group of helicopters, five of them, very large and very low. They came from the northwest. Maybe coming from Fort Indiantown Gap. I think there are soldiers there. I think I remember someone telling me that once.

They passed over, very low, and the air shook around me. The oats trembled as they rested softly against my hand. The helicopters moved to the south, toward the smoke.

I am wondering more about Mike today. All day long I expected to see him, but I did not.

AFTER DINNER, AND AFTER Jacob and I had finished our work, I went to the porch for a while to sit and pray. Hannah and Sadie had returned with the washing in the early afternoon, and after it was hung to dry, they busied themselves in the kitchen, talking earnestly about something I could not hear.

My prayers were selfish, out there on the porch, but we must pray when our hearts are struggling. Soldiers in Lancaster. I cannot remember such a thing, not in any of the stories from my father, or for generations.

I will admit that my soul was troubled. I wish that it was not so, because I know that God's purpose for all of us is good, and that God's Providence is all around us, even in the recent hard years.

But when the skies bear machines of war, and there are stories that sound like times of trial from the past, I confess that

I am not at ease. I think of what I know of war, from stories I have heard. I think of what I know from times of famine and hardship, from the struggles that even we simple folk have had to endure, from the times of flight and martyrdom, and I wonder about our own strength.

The feel of this is so very terrible, Lord, and so very different from what I would have thought. Lord, give me the strength for whatever I must bear, I prayed, and other things like that.

This is where my soul was, as I sat on the bench on the porch, the strong, strange heat of a late September day still heavy in the air.

And then Sadie nestled next to me on the bench, settling in like a falling leaf.

She was quiet and still next to me, asking nothing, but her head rested soft on my shoulder.

I opened my eyes and turned to her. We did not speak for a moment.

"I'm not afraid, Dadi," she said.

"Oh," I said. "You are not?"

"No," she said, looking at me as she can sometimes. It is as if you are made of glass, when she looks at you that way. Like she is seeing something through you. "No, I am not."

She rested her forehead against my shoulder again, and pressed it against the fabric of my shirt. A little tremble went through her, like a shudder on a cold morning, though the air was still hot.

"But if you are, it's all right." And she whispered into the blue fold of my shirt, "It's going to be so hard."

September 28

Sabbath worship was good yesterday. I felt it strengthen me, and was very thankful for the blessings of God's mercy in this strange time.

Such a busy day today. Still so hot, so hot for so late in September.

Isaak Stolfutz came by in the early evening, after dinner, as the heat of the day still hung in the air. He is a short man, lean and hard, with short legs and long arms. God made the Stolfutzes for farming, he likes to say. We talked a little about oats, and about the harvest. But mostly, we talked about what he was hearing from his neighbors.

The Smiths were on about one hundred and forty acres, a family of five. Bill and Donna, hardworking people, they are. I see them now and again, and they're loud and boisterous and friendly. Bill is from Alabama or Arkansas originally, I think. Someplace like that, and you can't miss that whenever he speaks. They moved up here to be near to Donna's parents when they got older, and their farm shares a fence or two with Isaak.

He was speaking with Bill this morning, but most of what he hears are only rumors. They had some power, their smallest generator worked, but they were being careful with gas. No power in most of the gas stations made getting fuel very difficult. Their refrigerator had failed, and so they had eaten from it for a few days. In their basement, a chest freezer held much of the beef they had kept for themselves after slaughtering a steer. They were carefully keeping it frozen, running it on that little generator for a few hours at a time, and thankful to God that it remains working. So many do not even have that.

But the corn could not be harvested, because the harvesters were dead things. And the Smiths' fields, always so carefully maintained, would soon show signs of being untended.

And then there were the things they had gotten from the Giant in Lititz. Bill had ridden there on his bicycle, and said the store was struggling. Cash only, no checks, no credit, but that was all right with Bill, because they always kept a reserve of money for emergencies. Much of what he got were frozen foods, good for a few more days. The manager at the Giant was practically giving it away, because it would soon spoil. Most of the meat had been a few days without refrigeration, and so much of it had already gone bad.

The shelves were pretty much emptied, but there were still some things left.

Bill had also gotten as many canned items as he could, to supplement what he and Donna always kept around. They had much they canned and preserved themselves, a full and stocked larder. With the cattle, and their gardens, and the chickens, they were fine. But their hired hands were having trouble getting there, and work was being left undone.

"Bill is a thoughtful and resourceful man," said Isaak. "I haven't known him to be frightened easily. But he is worried about the harvest, and worried about what he hears on the radio." Isaak paused.

I asked what that was.

Isaak cleared his throat. "He hears that tens of thousands are dead, fallen from the skies. That ships at sea have foundered, tens of thousands more assumed lost. And crashes. And fires. And the hospitals can do much less now, so many more die. The army is moving to maintain order in the cities, but that already in some places things are bad." He paused.

"But even the radio station doesn't seem to know much. Mostly rumors and stories they have heard." Isaak paused again, and seemed to fold up a little bit.

I thought about this. "And in Lancaster? What does he hear?" I asked.

He told me that the National Guard is there now. Hundreds of soldiers, a company of soldiers, they say, supporting the police. A state of emergency has been declared, and the soldiers are driving around in their four-wheel drives with big speakers. Apparently there is martial law, but no one knows exactly what that means, other than that there are soldiers with guns everywhere.

Everyone in Lancaster seems to be doing all right so far. But the world is not just Lancaster. There are larger cities, places where there are no fields and farms nearby, and where there is more violence. Pittsburgh, apparently, is bad. And other farther places, things were beginning to get bad. The biggest cities, like New York and Washington and Baltimore and Los Angeles. Rumors of violence. But just rumors. "Who knows anything anymore," Isaak said. "It all feels like gossip, like none of it is real."

IN THE HOUSE, MIKE is sleeping.

He arrived on a bicycle in the late afternoon, when Jacob and I were not there, but were working with the men to bale hay at the Schrock farm. It was not a long wait, but when we returned, Mike was out on the porch, his face still red, his heavy body still wet with sweat.

Hannah had gotten him lemonade, a pitcher of it, and he had drunk much of it. He was exhausted, because from his house, the ride is about eighteen miles. Not that far, perhaps, but though Mike is a big man, and he may have been very strong as a young man, there is so much flesh on him now.

We have talked about this, his weight and his smoking, his need to get more exercise, but he had always just laughed at me and told me he'd rather drive.

As I saw him there, red as a pickled beet and spent, I chose not to mention those conversations.

He didn't come about the work. He had heard nothing, nothing since that night. No one had heard much of anything.

We sat for a while, and we talked.

"I'm scared, Jacob," he said, as he talked through what he was seeing in the town. "Everywhere soldiers, and the big stores are pretty empty now, the Stauffers, the Giant, and the Turkey Hills are closed, and nobody knows anything. Nothing. Nobody working, and everyone is milling around." As people talked, the rumors would spread, and then no one would really know what was going on, but everyone would be upset.

"There's talk about food maybe coming in, but no trucks, no nothing. Even the Central Market, well, you know," he said. "We don't even have that produce coming in from all of the farms around here. Figured some would come this last Tuesday. With nothing working, folks went there on Tuesday hoping for something, but there wasn't anything to have."

He said something like that, but he was tired and agitated, so he forgot himself as he sometimes did. There were a few words added in that I am glad the children did not hear.

I reminded him, softly, and he was apologetic.

IN THE NIGHT, IN the night as I write this, I can hear trucks. They are a long way away, but they are out there moving. My prayers today are for Mike, and for our broken world.

October 1

Warm today, still very warm. But the heat has changed again, and everything is moist and wet. The sky was gray and fat and thick with rain clouds that race across the sky, and the wind howled through the trees. It felt very violent, a day stumbling around like a drunken, angry man.

It is growing darker in the morning, as the days begin to shorten. I feel the darkness more, though my day begins as it always does. Prayer, and then out to the barn, to the feeding and the blessing of work for the day. But I look around, and the glow that once rose from the south is still gone.

I remember that I did not like it, that in my morning prayers I would often ask the Good Lord to still my fears about it. There, or so my heart was moved sometimes, was the light of human sin. Bright and gaudy and wasteful, like the distant sound of overloud music.

I have not felt that way these last few days. I see darkness where once there was life and light, and my heart hurts. That darkness means that things are hard, and they do not seem to be getting better. It reminds me of the many thousands who are dead. It means people are still in darkness, and that they are growing more and more afraid and angry. And the English are people. They are God's children. They are my brothers and sisters. I think of Mike.

Mike went back home. He left early on Monday, said he had things to do, and the kids were with Shauna but he still wanted to be around.

Hannah made him some sandwiches, and gave him some water to fill his plastic bottles. Then he went off on that bicycle of his again, huffing and puffing. I could tell he was still tired from the ride here, but I could not help but think that maybe riding the bicycle was better for him that sitting in that truck all day long.

I think it must have been a difficult few days out in the world. Not for us. For us, life is much the same. But we are not the only people. I know that wherever Mike is, things are not easy. And there are many people like him.

I had picked beans for much of Monday, with Hannah by my side. They were a late crop, but the crops seem later and later every year with all of this warmth. Most of ours had already been canned and set aside by now, but there were still many vines yielding well, and we picked several bushels. We had the beans that normally we would sell, and we also had several crates of the strawberry jam that we had planned on selling at market over the fall. There was also a box of jerky and dried pork strips, all prepared before the storm to go downtown for sale.

That would have been some of our income for the fall, or we had planned it to be. But we do not know now what will be coming in the next weeks and months, and we know that we are in an emergency. The deacons had talked through it, and the word to all of us was that we would help as we can, with what food we can spare and with our skills.

That is as it should be.

I loaded the food on the wagon, and hitched up Pearl. Nettie doesn't like the wagon, and Pearl was always the bigger and stronger of the two. We took them over to where we had been asked by the Guard to bring them. The word of what was needed had come to Bishop Schrock, and then Jon and others had ridden it around the settlement. There were dozens of wagons there, and many menfolk. It was a little like a barn raising, in that way, but it didn't have quite the same feeling. There was a tension in the air, almost like the shimmer of the light on that terrible night.

I think it was seeing the trucks that made us feel differently.

The National Guard trucks came in the morning on Tuesday, eight of them, all in a line at the Schrock Farm.

The trucks were a strange and motley collection. All had that drab hardness of military vehicles, blunt and crude and purposeful. Most seemed to have been built for carrying men or supplies, but they felt irregular. I have watched columns of soldiers drive past, in their vehicles, all identical, as identical as their uniforms. It always feels very orderly, every soldier and every vehicle sharing the same appearance. It is, I think, what makes a soldier feel like he belongs to something. It is like the reason that we dress as we do, although it is such a terribly different order than our own.

But all of the vehicles today seemed different. I do not know anything about the ways of war, nor do I know trucks. I did notice, though, that the trucks that came seemed to be of all different sorts and sizes. They did not match.

One was the most different, with many wheels and a large and wicked gun mounted in a turret on the top. It did not seem like it was made to carry food. But it still ran, and so they were filling it up inside with everything that the community had gathered. It seemed strange to see it there, looking so fierce and terrible. And there we were, filling it up with jam and green beans and canned corn.

There were a dozen Guardsmen, most young, a few older. They helped load, working quietly and efficiently alongside us, their squad leader giving commands. Most of them worked with us. Two, though, remained on watch. They kept their rifles in their arms, which seemed peculiar to me.

As the work continued, Bishop Schrock took the squad leader aside and they talked. It was interesting to see his face. Something was upsetting him. It was not an easy conversation, whatever was being said. But they had moved away, many yards away, and they were not talking loudly, so I could not hear what they said.

I remained busy with those around me as we helped load the trucks. One man, his name was Jorge, was young and broad-shouldered, and had a serious manner about him. He had a wife and a daughter, and he told me their names, but I'm not sure I remember them well enough to write them down. He told me what he had been hearing and seeing. It was exactly what had been talked about at the Michaelsons' the other day.

Much was rumor, but he mostly knew what could be heard through National Guard talking. In the first few days, things had been calm for a while, but then there had been a panic in Philadelphia. Something had happened. I noticed that he did not say what.

"I totally get it, man," he said. "It's seriously scary." And he talked for a while about how much he understood why people were upset.

If you assume you can just go buy something, why would you have enough in your larder to keep you for a winter? Or even for a week?

And then suddenly you couldn't buy anything, and your credit card didn't work, and your debit card didn't work, and you couldn't go to the bank because the computers at the bank didn't work.

"People are freaked out when they don't know what's going on," he said. "And nobody knows what's going on. What are we even supposed to do? I can't work, 'cause my store can't sell anything. Who's going to buy a cell phone these days? And how would I even get paid?"

I asked him what he had seen, and he told me he didn't want to say. Then he thought for a few seconds.

"It's like the world just came to an end," he said, and paused. "Only we're all still here."

He talked more, about what his pastor said. I think he was Pentecostal. For years, there had been talk of the end of things. And about the Rapture, and about how the time was at hand. He seemed very upset when he talked about it, but it was an upset that went down deep.

I told him that I understood, but I think perhaps I do not. There are so many things I rely on, so many things that are just part of me, that I know are there and will be there. Hannah by my side. Sadie and her . . . specialness. Jacob. I take for granted that they are there, as I would the air in my lungs or the ground under my feet.

I assume the earth will yield, that what we plant will grow. There is always sweat, and the work is often not easy. But it will grow.

I assume the wood that I work will yield to my hand, to the craft that my father taught me. I assume that craft has worth, that it is vocation, and that it is useful and good.

And it is so with our little community. I assume that brothers will be there to help with the harvest, just as I know I will be there for them. I assume that sisters will be there to help prepare the house and to work side by side. It is how God made us, every one, to be a strength to one another.

Our community is, to me, what all the English had built was to him.

But now, for him, all of that is gone.

I DID NOT GO with the Guardsmen. Others did. Willis and Jon and Abram. They were to return by nightfall, but the days are shorter now.

They came back an hour after dark, a single truck returning with them in the dark of early evening. Funny, even a single truck is so easy to notice. A lonely patch of light, out in the nothingness.

I watched the lights of the truck, heard the faint hum of the engine as it moved through the quietness of our community. A mile or two away, they must have been. I knew I would talk with Abram the next day, as he came to help in our fields.

WEDNESDAY I HAD MUCH to do. It was a busy day, but by afternoon, most of the fieldwork was done. We do not have much land, after all, and the help others can provide makes light work of it.

Abram stayed after, and we sat on the porch. He and I talked about what he had encountered in Lancaster the day before.

Abram had ridden with the others in the lead truck. As they'd ridden along, he had talked with the squad leader, a staff sergeant. Sergeant Williams was a brick of a man, squat and solid and matter-of-fact.

It was a talk about money, at first.

There was just no way for the National Guard to pay us for the food and supplies we were giving. Orders were to provide supplies to Lancaster, at a couple of key locations. Our farms, and those few others that were still functioning, were where the supplies would be requisitioned.

But without any way to get money into a bank, or any way to use cash? What did it mean, to get paid?

"I'd thought about that," said Abram. "We're providing food, and it's an emergency. How can we think about money when there are those who are going hungry?"

Sergeant Williams had grunted. "That's what your Bishop said, when I tried to explain to him what I'd been told about compensation." He'd then shook his head. "I've heard that maybe the federal government is going to handle it, but everything we hear is bits and pieces. And how can they handle it, if there's no way to get money, and no way to transfer money? I could tell him what I'd heard, but nothing more."

Abram had then asked him if that was why Bishop Schrock was upset. The soldier had laughed, a sharp little bark. "No. No. Hard guy, that man, but he knew that was how things were. He'd asked me about martial law. About what it meant. About how it was being implemented in other places. About what I know. Damned if orders are that we're not to say, but hell. I'm still a citizen, and if you're giving us supplies with no idea when you'll get paid, I owe you what I hear. What I hear ain't good."

And then the Sergeant had stared at his boots for a while. "This is just a hell of a thing," he said. Then he had looked up. "You'd think people would work together. You folks know how to do that, right? But ain't nothin' working."

And then Abram himself went quiet for a moment, as he paused in the retelling. "And then he told me what he had heard from Philadelphia. From yesterday. A National Guard unit had been helping with the distribution of food from a church. There were too many people, and the crowd had swollen, and then they'd run out of food.

"But some in the crowd wouldn't believe it. Men were shouting, saying there was more food inside, that the soldiers were keeping it for themselves. Things had gotten ugly. The people began pushing, and shouting and screaming, and the soldiers had been trying to hold them back.

"But then there was a patter of shots, and one of the soldiers went down, and the crowd surged forward.

"Then the soldiers opened fire."

Abram went quiet again. "He told me there were at least a hundred dead. At least. Many of them women and children. And then he said they had heard more stories just like that."

And then he told me the soldier said, "It's all coming apart. Ain't no soldier signed up for killing kids."

But Lancaster was not like that, Abram said. It was peaceable. Tense, but peaceable. And there was still enough food, between the soldiers and the storekeepers and the emergency stores that every wise family had kept.

We talked for a while longer, about his kids, about the wild weather, about last Sunday's worship. It felt good to talk about other things.

October 2

It is dark in the house, and it is late, but I am awake. I am tired, because it was a long day of work, but I can't sleep now. It was the sound that woke me.

Once, twice, and then a patter of them. Gunshots, and not all the same gun. Some quieter pops, maybe a pistol, and then the deeper tone of a shotgun. It sounded like my father's gun, the old Remington he used for deer hunting. But no one hunts with a pistol, and it is too late in the night for hunting.

The shots were not close, maybe a mile off, and they were not really very loud. But I should not be hearing them at all.

Hannah did not wake, and I heard no movement from Jacob. It had been such a hard day, with so much work, that this was no surprise. I wished I was sleeping as they were. I lay there, but the sound had woken me from my dreamless sleep. I said a few prayers, prayers for whoever it was out there in the darkness. Then I lay there for a while, trying to return to slumber.

But I could not, as tired as I was. So I rose and lit the lamp and came downstairs. Sadie was there. She was sitting alone in her nightdress in the half-dark kitchen, holding a glass of water. I started a bit to see her, and my heart, already worried, stirred. If Sadie was up at night, that often meant bad things. But she seemed fine.

"Hello, Dadi," she said.

I asked her what had woken her.

"I heard the shots, Dadi. That's why you woke up, isn't it?"

I walked over behind her and held her shoulders for a moment. I told her that it was, and then I told her that she shouldn't worry, that they were far away.

"I'm not worried, Dadi," she said, with a very small smile. "But I think they aren't as far away as we'd like them to be."

I laughed a little bit, because it struck me as funny. Then I asked her how far away that was.

"So far away that we couldn't hear them," she said. "But we don't have a choice about what we hear. Sometimes we have to hear things even if we don't want to. Because they're there, aren't they, even if we don't want them to be."

She got up, and turned around, and rested her head for a moment against my chest. Then she stepped back a half step. "But it is quiet now. There will be no more sound tonight, I think."

She yawned, and her bright eyes were dimming with sleep. "I will go to bed." She stepped forward again, and I kissed her on the top of her head. "Good night, Dadi. Maybe you should write a little bit. It will help you sleep."

And so I have. Dear Lord, but I am tired now.

October 3

In the early afternoon, I went downstairs into the larder. With Sadie's help, Hannah had been working hard these last few weeks to be sure we were ready for the coming of winter, and she showed me what she had so far accomplished. That work does not only come in fall, of course. To prepare for winter, you need to be preparing the whole year. It is part of one's mind all year long. It must stay on your heart all of the time. And so it is with us. Always aware of what is coming.

The jars were there, hundreds of them. Corn and tomatoes, pickles and beets and beans, all neatly organized on the shelves. Each had been harvested in season, but our little patch of land has always yielded more than we need for the right now.

Hannah has been so competent at this, a good gardener, and a very diligent organizer. She is an excellent wife, she is, and I tell her so. She is a blessing.

Jacob and I have especially been helping her with the beef, the meat from the steer we slaughtered in August, and the two pigs. We had been storing it over at the Schrocks', in their large walk-in freezer. That compressor failed with everything else. That was a loss, a difficult one, not just for us but for everyone.

The community had agreed, years ago, that while all should not have refrigeration, it would be acceptable for us to share something. If we all had refrigeration, then it would tell us that we were each separate from one another. It would stir our pride, make us selfish, and let us pretend that we were each free of each other. But just one, shared among us all, owned by all of us together? That would be different.

That conversation happened well before we came, and a big part of it was where such a thing would go. It ended up on the Schrock farm. Some of the people who just cannot help but gossip do whisper about that, that it had to do with his pride and wanting to control it. Hannah has told me that some of the women say this. But I have talked with others. Bishop Schrock did not want it, and Mrs. Schrock did not want it, and for exactly that reason. But they had the space for it, and they are close to the center of all, and so that was that. It was how it needed to be.

It was a reminder, a reminder of just how reliant we had become on the English. We have cured and dried the pork and the beef. Salt and spices we had, and plenty of them. We had enough to share, as it was an old habit of mine going back to my father's house and the Order of my childhood.

There, refrigeration was forbidden. It was *hochmut*, prideful and arrogant. It would come up sometimes, but that Order was totally unyielding. What is pride is pride, as my father would say. And so for meat, things were different. It was put into soups that were canned. It was pickled. The taste of pickled pork still lingers in my mouth, and I will say that I never liked it very much.

But it was also saved by drying, and that I know as well as I know the feel of wood. There is something about jerky in particular that I have always loved. I love the chew of it, the rich salt of its flavor. It is so practical, so lasting, so good in its very simple way. There are few things more *demut* than a nice hunk of dried beef. That, I remember my father saying, too.

So we have dried meat, not just for ourselves, but enough to sell as we need to. The taste for jerky is another thing we share with the English, and for those that come to wander and wonder at simple folk, it's one of those things that they love to buy and take home. We sell it at our little stand, but it also has sold well enough in some stores in town, along with Hannah's preserves. It has been good for us in these years.

I do it differently from my father. Among that fellowship, the method was traditional. The long thin strips would hang on frames and trellises. I always thought they looked like meat socks hung out to dry. That was how it had always been done, and it did work, mostly. Sometimes birds would eat them, and sometimes the drying would not happen swiftly enough, and some of the meat would spoil.

But here, and with the permission of Bishop Schrock and consent of the others, I have used another method.

Between the house and the field are my drying houses,

three of them, built with my own hands. Funny little things they are, wooden cubes, looking a little like open chicken coops. Instead of chicken wire, they have large windows. I used glass windows, cast off from a nearby construction project. From the bottoms of the "coop" windows, three ramps of black-painted corrugated tin run from three of the four sides, facing south, west, and east.

The black-painted panels concentrate the heat of the sun, collecting it and increasing both the heat and the dryness inside the chamber. The concentrated hot air flows through the central chamber, and then up through a chicken-wire vent at the top. The meat—spiced by hand and cured for twelve hours—goes onto trays. It takes two full days, at most.

It is funny how you learn of these things. I did not learn it from my father, though he taught me to dry and prepare meat. It was in a conversation with a Baptist, years ago, which turned to our love of jerky. He shared with me what he had seen in Africa, how they dealt with their meat, and I confess that I had not heard of it. I should have, I think, but sometimes things that you should know dance just out of reach for many years.

These last few days, I have given out much salt and spices and advice to our neighbors. This is a good thing.

And it is also good, I think, to look into our larder, dry and cool. It is full of cuts and strips of beef and pork, all hanging like decorations, dried and ready to eat. It looks for all the world like a harvest of flesh, I thought, and though that was good to see, I found myself shivering when I thought those words.

But this will be food for my family for winter, when winter finally comes. And for some reason, I thought to something I had heard the day before. Of the refrigerators and the freezers at the Giant, of how they had tried to give away meat that could not be sold or kept. Of how much of that meat had spoiled, simply gone to rot. Hundreds of pounds of it, all of that effort, all of that work. It was such a terrible waste.

I am glad, now, for the hardness of my uncle and my father's uncompromising spirit. It does not happen often, I will admit. But sometimes I am glad.

IT WAS JUST A little after noon and the sun was high when Young Jon Michaelson came by, riding his mare. The heat was in the air, so Hannah offered him some lemonade, which he took gladly.

He was there bearing news. The shots we had heard were from the Smith farm. Bill Smith had woken to the sound of his dog barking. He had taken his shotgun to go investigate, and had startled three men breaking into their barn.

Two of the men just ran when they heard him, but the third man had a gun, and before he started running, he fired. Bill had fired back across the yard, and they had exchanged a volley. "No one was hit," said Jon, "but there are bullet holes in the front of the Smith house. And a window was shattered."

I asked if the police knew, and Jon said that one of the English neighbors of the Smiths had ridden his bicycle to tell them.

"But they are saying that there is not much the police can

do now for anybody, because there's no way to know what is happening soon enough. Most of the men on the farms now say that they are keeping watch together. Many are talking about forming a watch group."

What sort of group, I asked him.

"I saw the signs posted, as I was riding yesterday, and even more signs today. Asking for people to meet at the Stauffers tomorrow afternoon. Come and bring your guns, it said. Rally to protect your families, it said. The signs were all made by hand, but they all say the same thing. And I've heard my neighbors talking about it, too. They're talking about how important it is to be ready and organized to protect themselves if people come to take things. There just aren't enough Guardsmen, and the police can't be called in an emergency. I saw some of the guys I know from the area on the road yesterday, and they were all carrying their guns. I think every one of them is going to the Stauffers. It seems to be something that so many of our neighbors are doing."

I said that did not seem like a good thing to me, and he agreed.

"It feels like a nest of fire ants around here lately," he said. "All stirred up and angry about everything, ready to sting anything that comes close."

I agreed again.

GRACIOUS LORD, AS I prepare for sleep, I remember your Providence and grace and care. I remember how you watched over your people Israel, how you delivered them when they were slaves in Egypt. I remember my Savior, how he gave his life and his blood for all of us. I remember your love for all of us, written in that very same blood.

I remember all of these things, but I will admit that I am afraid. Sinner that I am, weak in the flesh, I cannot help but be afraid. Though I seek your peace and your calmness in all that I do, I find that my fears for my loved ones are strong. I am nothing, and I do not fear for myself. But Hannah and Sadie and Jacob are not me, and I love them so. I see that darkness is coming, and has come, and is all around us.

Care for them, Father. Watch over us. Give me your peace, that I might have the strength that is needed for those we both love.

In the Blessed Name of Jesus I pray, Amen.

October 4

The morning found the world again touched by a coolness, a blessed coolness. Not a chill, but an easing off. No longer summer, whispered the morning. No longer summer.

With the animals fed and breakfast eaten, I hitched Nettie up to the buggy and waited as Hannah readied herself and Sadie for worship. Jacob walked along the path, dressed neatly, or as neatly as he can be. He grows like beans on a vine, that boy does. His pants seem always too short, his broadening shoulders straining his dark jacket, his hat just a tiny bit too small.

I watched him, walking in the drive, aimless and thinking, kicking a rock through the dust. Still a boy, but not for much longer. I wonder, for a moment, about his running-around, about his *rumspringa*, just a few years away. How will he run around, if the English world is in tatters? I do not know.

Nettie sat patiently in the harness, and so I walked a little myself, pacing down the drive. I could see, here and there, a whisper of yellow in the leaves of the big oak near the gate. Not much yet, just a hint, like the first speckle of pepper gray in a man's beard. The rising sun played across the tree, catching it with that rich, warm morning light.

And there, in the air beneath the canopy of the oak, I saw a single bright yellow leaf. It was not falling. It hovered, whirling, floating and bobbing and moving. It did not fall. It refused to fall.

I watched it as it danced, defying the fall, a leaf that would not come to earth. It was magic, this leaf.

A soft morning breeze rose up, and the golden leaf lifted upward, arcing back toward the branches that had cast it down. Like a fallen angel, repentant, straining back toward heaven.

I knew what I was seeing, even though I could not see it.

Attached to the leaf, defying my sight, beyond my human seeing, there was a single silver thread. That cord was there, though I could not see it, strong as steel, light as air. I knew this. It was woven by a spider, and fixed to the leaf, and fixed to the tree.

That is why I was seeing a leaf that would not fall. I knew this.

But it still seemed magical. Just like everything in our world.

When she came out, I showed it to Sadie, who always loved such things. She hugged me, and planted a little kiss on my cheek.

"Hope, Dadi," she whispered in my ear.

WORSHIP TODAY WAS LONG, and made the longer by Bishop Schrock's preaching. But that it felt long did not mean that it felt unspiritual. We sang with fervor, and listened to his preaching, and even though it was long, it felt needed. We were hungry for it, for the comfort of our worship, for the songs.

He talked and he talked, and his voice was dry and it did not vary. But there was something different in the tone and the way that he was speaking. Or perhaps there was not, and it just seemed so.

He always does talk about the importance of staying strong in the spirit of calmness, of being dutiful and diligent in pursuit of peacefulness, of how important the many rules of the Order are for giving our lives joy and balance. I have heard the same words from Bishop Schrock in every sermon he has preached since Bishop Beiler became too weak to preach.

He is like the sun rising in the morning, or the full moon coming in its turn. Always the same.

But today, perhaps I needed to hear it in a way that I usually do not. When the world is wild and inconsistent, sometimes simple and consistent are a comfort.

He was nearly finished speaking—I think—when the helicopters came over. They have been flying these last few days, back and forth, in threes and fours. Great big helicopters. One of the neighbors told Joseph Fisher that they were carrying thousands and thousands of MREs, which is some kind of preprepared food that the army uses. The same food that is in the columns of trucks that move and rumble through the night.

They were low and huge and flying close together, and the room shook with the thunder of them. You could feel it in your skin, in your body and bones, the beating of those blades against the air.

It throbbed like the beating of your heart in your ears when you have been running. It was the whole world. It was so loud that Bishop Schrock stopped talking. That takes some doing.

We all stood still for a moment, and then another, as nothing could be heard or said or sung. They passed, fading off into the south. There was a moment of silence in the fading of the sound, as if the room was holding its breath, as if all of us were listening for another sound. What more might come? What sounds of violence would follow?

And then the Bishop began talking again, without missing a single word, as if nothing had even happened.

It is moments like that, I think, that I most appreciate him.

WE RODE BACK TOGETHER, after the day of worship at the Schrock farm. It was good, without question, to spend that time together. There was much talking, much speculation. There is worry. Nothing seems to be changing, at least not for the better.

In the buggy, with the sound of the hooves and the smell of horse, we were all silent after a long worship.

Home we went, and then prepared to go over to see the Fishers.

• • •

JOSEPH MET US AT the gate, along with young Rachel, who called out to Sadie and Rachel and their five, plus the older Rachel pregnant again, they have been blessed and fruitful.

The three boys hollered out to Jacob, and off they all went running, off toward the creek at the edge of the Fisher place. We brought food in, and Hannah settled in to chat with Rachel in the kitchen as the food was readied, while Joseph took me around to see how the painting of the storm damage had been going.

Sadie and young Rachel went off walking and talking, as they do. It was good to see that, good to see her at ease. She was always so, I don't know, so *awkward* around other children. When she was little, oh, it was fine. But she would say such strange things to them sometimes, and children can be so . . . hard. So hard on those who are different.

The other girls, they have come by less and less over the last year, since she had worsened. She does not run with the gang, laughing and playing and talking, because they did not know how to be with her. And when she told Fannie Hostetler about her nose, before she even broke it?

Fannie took it as spoken from jealousy, or spite. How else was she to understand it? So the circle closed, and Sadie was outside of it. Until the fall from the horse. Then they were not angry. There was fear, I think.

But Rachel was always there for her, even when Sadie herself was not really there, though it was sometimes hard. I could see it with my own eyes, how she was the only one remaining, but it was also in being with her and listening even when what was said was strange and hard. Hannah told me so.

But the clusters of girls who would move in clouds, passing by on their skates? She was not part of that. She was too intense.

So it is good to see her with Rachel.

The tree damage to the house was almost invisible, and the new coat of paint, purchased before all of this began, makes the house look perhaps even better than it did before the tree fell.

The remnants of the tree now sit neatly stacked, standing off a ways from the house, several cords' worth. It was a big and healthy tree, and when that wood has cured, it will be good for a few winters of heat from their woodburning stove.

The boys had cut most of it, over these last few days, splitting and sawing and preparing it, dragging the leafy branches off to a nearby stand of trees.

"Good work for boys," Joseph had said. "Keeps them busy and out of mischief."

But then our talk turned, as it does so much these days, to what we were hearing from the outside. I shared with him what I had heard in my conversations with Young Jon Michaelson, and he listened patiently, nodding in agreement. When I had told him all of what I had heard, he said, "Yes, that's what Young Jon told me, too."

As hard as the story was, I laughed a little bit. "And you didn't think to stop me?"

"No," he said. "Because the story as you tell it is just a little bit different. And I like to hear that."

He told me, then, other stories he had heard. Joseph is a listener, and I know he made his way to some of the English stores just to hear what was going on. "I was told that there are fires in Boston, fires that have been burning for a week in some of the big buildings there. They cannot put them out, and the rains haven't been enough to extinguish them, and they are spreading."

"What else have you heard?" I asked.

"That they are going to begin to close the roads, to make it so that only the army can travel, and that they are impounding fuel. One man at the Giant . . . Don Samuels, I think his name is . . . was shouting to anyone who would listen that the army was going to take all of the guns so that no one could fight them. He was also yelling about how the Sun storm was really just a secret weapon to give the government an excuse to take away guns."

"Really?" I asked. "Was anyone listening to him?"

"Some were listening politely, and a couple intently, but most of the people were trying to ignore him."

"Is that what they're calling it now?" I asked. "Sun storm?"

Joseph thought for a minute. "I've heard that. And some are calling it the Big Carrington, I think because some guy called Carrington had seen a storm like that before. And I remember hearing it called Lucifer's Night, because of the lights. And the Second Flood. Because it wasn't a flood of water, but of heaven. A lot of people seem to think that it was God's judgment on man. But most just call it the Blackout."

I asked him what he thought.

He shook his head. "I don't know. It doesn't fit with anything that I read about in the Bible, not if I'm honest with myself. A lot of people are trying to make it that way, make it fit with something in Revelation, but it doesn't feel right to me."

I told him I felt the same way. Sometimes, a storm is just a storm.

Then we talked about the Johansons. As bad as it was before with them, it is ten times worse with them now. They were struggling. He could not easily work with his hand so badly burned, and he was not taking it well. Another neighbor said he is drinking even more, and they are fighting all of the time. He hears them screaming at each other, even across the fields, and Joseph is worried.

"I don't even know if they have enough food," said Joseph.

I AM AWAKE AGAIN, and it is deep in the night. I woke up, because Sadie woke me. "Dadi," she whispered in my ear. "Come and see, Dadi." Her eyes, bright and intent, watching my face. Her head moving slightly, changing perspective, as she does when she pays attention to you. Like a little bird, I always thought, or maybe the way that a praying mantis bobs and shifts to see.

I took care not to wake Hannah, and we went downstairs. Sadie is so quiet as she walks, as if her feet barely touch the earth. We stepped out of the house, and in the clear night sky the heavens were gently dancing with faint light.

My heart leapt to my throat for a moment.

But Sadie seemed unmoved, except for a little smile. "It isn't anything, Dadi," she said. "They are far away this time. I love the way they move and dance. So beautiful, aren't they?"

I agreed, because they were very beautiful, as they had been the first time we had seen them. We watched for a while. There was no electric smell in the air, and my hair did not rise in hackles as it had before. This was not the same, and I thanked Jesus for it.

The air was cool, almost with a bite in it, the coldest it had been in a while. The sky billowed, sheets of light hung on the sharpness of a crescent moon. I told Sadie that they were called aurora, as I had told her before, but she was lost in the sight. I do not know if she heard me.

And as we stood there and watched, there were gunshots again from far away. One gun, very faint, *crack crack crack crack*. And a pause, and again it sounded, *crack crack crack crack*. And again, *crack crack crack crack*. Sadie noticed, but she just watched the skies, and smiled.

But as beautiful as the sky was, it was hard to hear that sound. I prayed that it did not mean anyone was being hurt.

The sound of shots continued, a faint tapping on the door of the night. After a while, Sadie and I went inside, because it was getting too cold.

October 5

The morning was sharply colder than yesterday, perhaps forty degrees, and I wore my jacket and my coveralls as I tended to the horses. Jacob was out with the chickens, and I watched him struggling with his old coat from last year as he worked. The sleeves were halfway up his arms, and it was too tight for him to do much in it. Not that he noticed or complained.

"I think you'll need a new coat soon," I said to him. He just grinned back. I wondered if Hannah had enough fabric.

In the garden, Sadie was watering and putting in the broccoli seedlings, now that we are hoping that the temperature is finally cool enough. We have had such trouble with our fall crops these last years, with the warmth, but if we stagger them and are careful, they will still yield.

When the morning chores were done, we settled in the kitchen to eat breakfast, as always, together as a family. The kitchen was so warm, and where that warmth was unwelcoming in the height of the summer, it felt wonderful this morning. Few things are more like home than a kitchen in winter, as my mami used to say.

Later in the morning, I heard from Young Jon about the gunshots last night, as he rode by with news. He does that more and more now, and it is good that he does. We need to hear what is happening, and his telling is the best way.

He had talked to Joseph Fisher, and Joseph had told him that the shots had come from the Johanson place. Mr. Johanson had been drinking, drinking all day, and there had been fighting and shouting from the house in the afternoon. Then Mrs. Johanson had gone with the children. They had walked, leaving the house on foot to go to a friend's house a few miles away, Jon was not sure who. And they were carrying a bunch of things with them, and she was pulling a child's wagon filled with food and supplies.

The house was silent after the fighting, but when the aurora came, he went outside with his rifle. The Johansons always had many guns, Joseph had told me, and the worse things got with the family business, the more guns he seemed to have. A couple were for hunting, but most were not.

Then he was shouting, shouting drunken curses at the sky, and firing his rifle over and over again at the heavens. He screamed and screamed, Jon said, and for ten minutes he howled terrible things at the sky.

It was very frightening for the Fishers next door, said Jon, because you do not know where the bullets will go when a drunken man is firing wildly.

And this time, there were no police to call. There was no way to call anyone else.

The Fishers stayed inside their house during the shooting, and moved to the rooms downstairs and on the other side of the house. When the gunfire stopped, and stayed stopped for a while, Joseph went out to see what was going on. He looked around for a while, in the fields. He went to the house. It had been open. There were many things smashed, and there were a few bullet holes. But he couldn't find Mr. Johanson.

In the morning, he went to talk with other English neighbors. The last Jon heard, there was talk of a search party to look for the elder Johanson.

"Are you going to have supplies ready for the Guard tomorrow?" asked Jon. It was Tuesday again, and the Guard was going to try to bring more food from our community and others to supplement the other materials they were bringing in.

I told him that I would be ready, and that we would set aside some of the meat, and some of the fall peas and lettuce from the garden. And then, as I was about to say that we could give away some of the strawberry and blackberry preserves, and our raspberry jam, the words stilled themselves before they reached my tongue. Though we had much more of them than we could ever use, I could not say this, not yet. Those preserves were the things that we had planned on selling. Or, rather, these were the things that Hannah was planning on selling. We would need to talk, Hannah and I.

So I did not speak.

It is one of the things that I have learned, over the years with Hannah. A wife makes a far better helpmate if you remember to ask her before doing something.

And then Jon was off, shouting farewell as he rode off toward other farms.

HANNAH AND I TALKED for a while after dinner tonight. It began with conversation about the larder, about how prepared we were to face the winter. We had talked a little bit about it yesterday, for a moment or two, but as the day wound down today and the dishes were done, she settled in reading. I wrote in my journal, and read a little bit myself, but finally moved to sit nearer to her. I told her about what Young Jon had said, about how I might want to go to Lancaster with the men in the truck tomorrow.

"It would be good to see with my own eyes how the town is doing," I said, and she nodded.

Then I asked about the preserves. "I know you were going to sell them," I said. "And I know there are no clients for a while for my woodwork, we may need the money. But we have so much, and there is such a need."

She looked down for a moment, as she does whenever she is thinking.

"I think we need to give some," she said. "But we do not know how long this will last. We need to think about how we might be called upon to give again, how there will be needs beyond our own that we must be prepared to meet as the days grow shorter."

She smiled a little, and cocked her head in a way that always makes me want to be nearer to her. "You know how I get when we're not prepared for guests who are coming to visit. We must have a little extra, and work just a little harder."

I nodded, and agreed. A wise wife is such a blessing.

October 6

Cold again this morning. Couldn't have been more than forty-five degrees when I woke in the darkness. I worked the morning, and then as I was getting ready to ride to the Schrocks', I saw Isaak arriving with his wagon. By his side was Bill Smith, who'd ridden along. To talk with me, apparently.

Bill was a big man, with hands like hams and a ruddy face. His face is big and flat, and set into it is a smile filled with big teeth. He smiles a great deal. He was even smiling as he told me about how things are hard. He was one of the fortunate few who had some equipment still working, a generator and a couple of freezers. But they were running low on fuel. He had a tank he kept on the farm for fuel, and that would last for a while, but the military had been requisitioning gas, and what little could be had was at outrageous prices. So he could see that his stocked freezer full of meat wasn't going to be good for much longer. He'd heard from Isaak what we'd done with our meat, and remembered buying some of our jerky at the roadside stand, and wanted to see if he could buy or barter for some of the salts and spices we had.

I asked him if he'd ever cured meat before, and he grinned and said that he had. And that he loved our jerky. With his big teeth, I can see how he would like jerky.

We talked for a while. Money right now is not very helpful. So he would bring us apples from his orchard, a couple of bushels. I think that would be fine, but I went back in to the kitchen to talk with Hannah about it.

She was fine with it, too, and so I came back out and we shook hands on it.

He seems like the kind of man whose handshake matters.

THE MILITARY TRUCKS ARRIVED at the Schrock farm, only three of them this time. We loaded them up, close to full, working carefully and intently together. The work was done quickly, and then I settled in to the first of the trucks, along with Isaak and three Guardsmen.

We moved along the roads toward Lancaster, passing out of our little community and going along one country road after another. We passed farm after farm, and as we moved beyond where I usually venture, I was struck by the absence of work. Nothing was happening on most of the land, even though the crops were almost overfat and nearly past the time of harvest.

The harvesters and combines were not busy. The tractors were not moving. There was no activity on most of the farms. It was still and quiet.

I asked the driver—his name was James—if there were any among the English farms still operating, if the Guard were picking up flour or anything else from them. He said he didn't know, but that he hadn't seen much of anything.

"I think there was a bakery open, I think. Or a couple of them, smaller ones, the ones selling organic bread. But the big mills are still not running, so, you know, like, that's not been easy. Getting the flour to the little shops is just really hard, and once you get it there—well, shoot. It's just hard."

I said that I was sure that it was, and then asked him how the city was holding up.

"Doing okay so far, I guess. Nothing like the bigger towns. At least there's farms and food around here. It's gotten real bad other places, that's what we hear. I mean, so many people got a couple of days of food, or maybe some were good for a couple of weeks. I mean, really, if you eat your way through the fridge in five days, and then you were smart enough to have emergency food good for a week, you'd be doing better than most folks."

So more people are coming for food now, I asked.

He grunted. "Yeah, you could say that. Not at all like those pictures you always used to see of Africa or nothing, but— yeah. Oh, everything is fine here so far, though folks do worry. But this thing makes me worried about my mom and dad. Shoot, I don't even know how they're doing, so far away and all. Desperate people do stupid things."

He looked out the window. "People know that there can't be any looting, but they still do it. Like some people went into the Walmart over near Elverson, busted in the doors with a truck. They weren't even taking food. They were taking big-screen TVs. Who even needs big-screen TVs now? And even when they know looting is a crime, and with emergency powers and martial law in place, they know what that means. Why would you even do something so stupid?"

Because it seemed like he wanted to talk about something else, I asked him where his parents were, and he told me that they'd moved to California a couple of years back, buying up a cheap house that had been foreclosed on.

"I don't even begin to know how I'd talk to them. Nobody's Skyping, right? And none of the phones work, right? Not cells, not landlines, and everything's a mess. Just gotta pray, I guess."

I asked how old they were.

"My dad's, what, sixty-two now. And his health isn't that great. Problem with his heart, you know, and he takes all of these pills. I don't know what's even happening with that." .

We talked, then, for a while, about our dads, as the trucks rumbled slowly southward.

As we got closer to town, coming down Oregon Pike, we began passing neighborhoods, developments out near the edges of Lancaster. I'd been there before, many times before. For the most part, it looked as it always looked.

But in one development, a row of houses were blackened and burned. And I noticed that there were piles of trash out by the fronts of some of the houses, garbage piling up, with no one to collect it. The piles were not large, but the neat

lines of houses had not been marked by them before. I wondered what would become of them.

And when I had come through the neighborhoods before, driven to market by Mike, there were never any people
around. It was the funniest thing, about the English, about
how all of their neighborhoods are always so nice and filled
with things, and yet they seem to have no people in them
at all.

What I noticed, as we drove through, was that today the
neighborhood was filled with people. Kids, some milling
around, most playing. Adults sitting or talking in circles, or
busying themselves at the height of the day, as the warm sun
drove out some of the chill.

There were no moving cars, but there were people on bicycles, some of which were pulling carts full of things. On
some corners, there were parked military vehicles.

As we passed, all eyes came up. We were watched as we
went, heads turning, mouths moving to share some thought
or another.

We arrived at the Market, and there were plenty of people
waiting, and many soldiers. Other trucks were arriving, most
of them military, but some of them civilian.

The distribution was orderly, despite my worries. People
seemed to be getting along and helping each other. There was
a feeling of purpose in the air, but there was talking and even
the occasional laugh.

It was a funny thing, because in my mind I had assumed it
would be something else. Somewhere, in the last week, I had

thought it would be a teeming throng, like the panicked mob in Pittsburgh that Jorge had told me about.

But it was not that. The city was intent. It was focused. People were doing what they needed to do, and yes, there were many soldiers around. But it felt neighborly. It felt like people were pulling together, like they knew each other. The feeling was one of common purpose, like when we gathered at the Fisher house to help rebuild, or when we work together for the harvest. That whispering fear that it would be a madhouse was just a lie.

As I reflect back on the day, I wonder how much of that came from my own fears of the English. Yes, I would not choose their life. But so much of my growing up was in a place where they were not viewed as neighbors, but as dark and terrible and spiritually dangerous. In my heart and through my faith, I do not feel this to be true, but it is difficult to entirely lose that fear once it is planted.

October 8

These have been two difficult days.

Late on Wednesday morning, I rode over to the Fisher place to talk with Joseph. I had heard in the morning that they had found Tom Johanson's body, deep in his unharvested cornfield.

Joseph was still working the soil for one of their fall gardens when I arrived, expanding it with the plow. I walked by his side as he drove his team, and he talked.

"It was a little hard getting the word out for a search party," Joseph said, over the loud clink and clatter of the harness. "But we did, sending out riders and bikers to see what folk were willing to come out. I think that I was hoping all along that our prayers would be answered, and that we'd just find Tom sitting on his porch, apologetic and promising never to do it again." It had been that way, so many times.

But not this time.

"A couple of men brought their hunting dogs, with the idea that we could use them to help track, but as it turned out, it was hardly necessary. He was at the far corner of his field, furthest from my house, and the crows had found him first. Once we saw them, all circling there, we knew exactly what we would find. It's like the scripture says: 'Where the vultures gather.'"

I asked if he took his own life.

"It was that way," said Joseph. "He had taken a round to the head. It was not easy to see. And yes, he had been drinking, and yes, drunkenness and guns are a bad mix. But I do not think it could have been an accident like that with a rifle. So, yes, he killed himself. Perhaps it would be better to say that his drunkenness took his life. He was like two different people. Quiet and thoughtful and with a strong wit, when he was sober. But he was not sober often, especially these last few years. That other Tom took them both."

And his wife? How is she?

He shook his head. "I told Julia," said Joseph. "Lord help me, I had wondered if it would fall to me. Tom had fewer and fewer friends over these last few years. He'd always been private, but as things got harder and harder on the farm, he had turned away from everyone. I think he spent all of his time on his computer, talking with other people who were as angry as he was. But they were not friends, not in any way that mattered. They had no family nearby. And he and Julia had stopped going to church after that fight they had with another family there.

"So yes, I told her. Went over to the Turner farm with a deputy who'd come out to help coordinate the search. She and Bess Turner were always close, or so Rachel tells me. It was hard, but who else could do it? She did not take it well."

I said that it didn't surprise me. It was such a hard thing.

"She," Joseph began, and then he coughed, as if his throat had closed a little bit. He started again. "She could not stop screaming and crying. She had trouble standing. Bess had to take her upstairs, and she was still crying out when I left. It was as if she could not hear anyone anymore. I worried that it might be that way, but it was still hard to see. The children are still little, and it is so . . . hard for them to understand such things. I . . ."

And he stopped talking for a while, as the team pulled and the plow bit deep, and the rich smell of turned earth filled the air.

I did not press him.

For a minute, and two, we walked in silence, only the sounds of horses and earth filling the air.

Then he told me that they had buried Tom on his property, right out by the property line. There seemed nothing else to do.

"I said a couple of prayers over him," Joseph said. "I do not think he would have minded."

October 9

Thursday in the morning, Jon came riding by, with some more news. It was not good. The body of a man had been found by the roadside, near a field by Clay Road. He had been shot, many times.

No one knew who he was, and he did not seem to have any identification.

A sign had been hung around his neck. It said: LOOTER.

The men who found him buried him, even before the sheriff got there.

Before he rode off, Jon told me that no one around there remembered hearing shots. Or if they did, they were not saying.

Two men dead in two days. It is a difficult thing, and feels like an ill wind.

October 10

I woke early today, before the sun, before the cockcrow. The moon was still nearly full, and low in the sky, and the faint light cast our room in a gentle blue. Like the air in the house, it felt cool and sharp, but the bed was warm. I lay there, in the warmth of our bed, and my mind played out against the events of the last two days.

An ill wind.

I rolled to my right, to look at Hannah. I will do that sometimes, when I wake in the night and she is sleeping. I'll just lie there in the silence, and in the darkness, and look at the shadow softly breathing next to me.

Her face was lit by the moon, cool and ghostly.

Her eyes were open.

"Good morning, Jay," she whispered. "You can't sleep?" Only she calls me Jay. Only she ever. It isn't really my name, but I have never minded.

I told her that I could not.

"I can't either. I was dreaming about Tom and that man.

It wasn't a good dream, so I woke up." Her voice was even and matter-of-fact, but in the half-light I could see that she was distressed.

"It has been hard," I said. "To have death moving so close, so near to us."

"And especially with Tom. I know they had struggled, but . . ." She paused. "I just don't know what it would be to lose you. Not just because you'd died, but because you'd died inside even before that. I just don't know how such a thing would feel."

I told her that I wasn't planning on dying.

She curled in closer, and closed her eyes, and nestled on my shoulder.

"I am so glad that God brought you to me, Jacob," she whispered.

We lay there for a while, and she fell asleep again. I did not. I lay there as she slept, until the moon's faint light gave way to the coming day.

BILL SMITH CAME BY again later in the morning, riding his bicycle. This time, he came to thank me for the salts and the spices.

On the back of the bicycle he had fastened a couple of apple pies, and a bag of apples from his orchard. Wrapped in bloody wax paper were also a couple of good cuts of venison from a deer he'd shot just the day before. It was a generous trade for the spices, but this was no surprise. Bill was a generous man.

The apple harvest is still in full swing here, and I asked him how it was going. None of his machines were working, he replied, but the harvest was now proceeding by hand.

He said that some people from Lititz had come in a pickup, a bunch of people, all piled into the back of an old Ford that they had been able to get running. They'd helped much of the day with the harvest, picking and filling baskets. For their work? He'd fed them, then paid them in big bags of apples, and in slabs of bacon and pork from four pigs he'd slaughtered the day before.

"They still have food coming into Lititz," he said. "But those MREs are just god-awful stuff, and canned fruit gets real old, and there's only so much baked beans you can eat." He grinned. "*Hooo*, is that true."

I asked him if any of the other farmers around were doing the same thing, and he said that they were starting to get more and more folk coming out from the towns looking for work in the harvest in exchange for food.

"We've just got so much to do, and there's so many who don't have anything to do. It's still hard, though, getting the word out about what we need. Some of the stores are pitching up bulletin boards, though, where we can put up what hands we need and when. And if you go by 'em, you get men standing 'round and waiting for work. Guess that was the way it used to be, eh? Everyone working together, sharing stuff."

He grinned widely. "But y'all know that better'n pretty much anyone."

We talked a little bit about the man they'd found out by

the roadside. Bill thought there were folks around here who might have done it, but nobody was saying much of anything.

"Sometimes everybody helps everybody else, and then sometimes they think they're helping. Hate to see a man killed like a dog, but these are strange times."

I said that I couldn't help but agree.

After I asked, he told me that there was more news about the state of emergency. They had closed more of the interstates, and there was talk of a curfew.

"It ain't like nobody can do much moving around anyway, but it feels weird not to be able to at all. Folks don't like being told what they can and cain't do, 'specially when it comes to where you can go. All the gas stations are dry anyway, and what gas folks do have they ain't sellin'. Guess that doesn't mess with y'all at all, though."

I said that it did, perhaps more than he might think. If it hurts a neighbor, it messes with us.

"Yeah, I'd figure you'd think that way."

IN THE AFTERNOON, I did as Joseph had done. We had many seeds left for planting . . . broccoli and lettuce, cabbage and cauliflower . . . and though our usual garden was plenty for us, I expanded the plots. Pearl was her usual patient, solid self as we turned the soil, and Nettie remained back in the stable.

It is later than I would typically plant, but even if the seeds do not take, it feels like we will need to cultivate more in the

coming year. In the house, Hannah and Sadie worked together, preparing the pies that we would bring to the worship
tomorrow.

After a while, Hannah sent Sadie out to bring in the clothes
from the line, which they'd handwashed instead of taking over
to the Stolfutzes. It worked almost as well, and it took less
time than loading up and riding.

"It looks to rain tomorrow, Dadi!" she shouted out to me.
"It's good you're getting the soil turned today!"

And I suppose it is good. A little rain will help set in the
seeds.

COME SUNDOWN, IT WAS not as cold as it had felt in
the morning, a breeze had come up. The wind was blowing
from the south, gusting and pulling at my clothes, snatch-
ing at my hat. It caught leaves from the trees, and here and
there, they would dance through the air. Little shadows, flit-
ting across the rose-colored sky.

It made a very lovely sunset, as the clouds moved swiftly
across the sun. Under the front porch, the rain-stick is droop-
ing down. It felt like a storm.

October 11

When I woke, the wind was stronger still, and the temperature was very noticeably warmer. The clouds were heavier, and the rain came in gusts and squalls. The morning's chores were wet and cold, and the animals seemed anxious as we fed them.

Worship would be at the Beilers' today, and though we usually would not have worship on this Sunday, everyone last week had felt that we should gather for prayer and preaching and singing. It felt even more vital for us to be together in such a way, and Isaak had agreed that he would preach, even though it was not his turn.

That would be good to hear, because Isaak always had a way of finding the best grace in any sermon. Everyone had agreed last week that it would be a good thing.

But last week, we did not know that today would be a squalling mess of rain. It makes it feel more important, some-how, when we make the effort to gather together even though the weather is rough. I was also remembering that time two years ago, when the snows came fast and thick, and Nettie had struggled mightily. It had not been easy to get home that day.

I don't think Nettie feels quite as positively about worship when the weather is bad. Certainly not as I brought her out from the barn.

Nettie seemed skittish as I hooked her to the buggy, much more so than usual. We piled in as quickly as we could, and Jacob sat up front with me as Hannah and Sadie nestled in the back. Just a few moments, we were in the rain before we'd secured the side curtains, but the rain fell in heavy sheets. I wore my long coat, but it was not quite enough to keep the wet out. Warmer though it was, the wind still bore a chill, and I felt it through my clothes.

We rolled down the drive, and onto the road, and began making our way to the Beilers' for the worship. The rain lashed against the buggy, beating angrily against the sides. With each gust, and each blast of rain, the buggy rocked and creaked. "Tall like a sail," shouted Jacob, and he was right.

Water sprayed in around the edges of the rain curtains, and Hannah and Sadie moved more toward the center of the buggy.

There was a flash of lightning, close by, and the thunder came in a great concussion right afterward. Nettie started, just a little, and I reined her back. We all started, in fact, just a little.

It was clear that this was a strong storm, and the further we got out into it, the more I wondered at the wisdom of continuing. It was a long ride.

When we got there, Hannah and Sadie ran inside, carefully sheltering the pies that they had baked. Isaak, who was waiting in the drive, shouted out to tell us to park over by their bigger barn and lead Nettie inside. Normally, we'd have put her in the field, but as the wind snarled and howled and the rain beat down, that did not seem kind.

"Too rough to leave the horses outside! Quite a storm!" We got her unhitched, and inside, and then made our way to the smaller barn, the place we gathered to worship whenever we were over at the Beilers'.

Some were there ahead of us, but most had not arrived yet. Others came eventually, all soaked to the skin, and we settled in to listen to the first of the sermons.

Young Bill Stolfutz was offering it, and he'd been selected to preach only just last year. He tried, he did, every time, and we'd sit and listen because even in the simplest effort, you can hear God speaking. Usually.

But not today. The rain hammered and rattled and shook the metal roof of the barn, and the wind battered the walls of the barn, and our ears were full of the sound of it. Bill has never been the loudest man, and it is one of the things I appreciate about him, but his voice just could not carry over the roar.

Still, he did what was his duty, and preached, and we could tell this because his mouth was moving.

Then we sang, and sang some more, and then there were prayers. We sang with more vigor, so as to be heard, and our voices seemed to mingle with the thunder and the drumming of the rain.

When it was Isaak's time to preach, he raised up his voice so that he could be heard, even though the roar from the roof had not diminished.

Mostly heard, to be honest. His sermon was good, about the rain, about the need to hold together no matter what storms came, to remain faithful and with our feet on the solid rock.

But Isaak did not preach long. As he was midway through the preaching, lights from a vehicle pulling in to the Beiler yard could be seen through the rain-spattered windows. A few moments later, three soldiers dressed in rain gear entered by the back, and one signaled the attention of Bishop Schrock.

There were words, not whispered but inaudible in the din, and Isaak stopped his preaching for a moment. Those gathered sat quietly, with little whispering and wondering. Bishop Schrock came forward to Isaak, and their heads drew close to each other, and they conferred.

When they were done talking, Isaak raised his voice to almost a shout so that all in the room could really hear him.

"These soldiers have come to tell us that they have heard there may be a hurricane coming up the East Coast, and it seems to be coming straight for us. They do not know how strong it is, or how strong it will be, or even how soon it will get worse. It is hard to tell in these days. But the radio reports from the military say it is a very strong storm."

There was murmuring around, as many of us still remembered Sandy, and how fiercely she had come through all those years ago.

Bishop Schrock chimed in, his deep voice booming. "It may not be safe to return home if we wait much longer, or if we continue on through our time of fellowship. We give thanks to our friends for bringing us this news and in braving the elements to tell us this, and we should act upon the news we have been given." He nodded to the soldiers, who nodded back.

We sang one more song, raising our voices together, but we only sang about half of the verses. Then, a prayer, and the womenfolk bustled to gather up what had been brought while the menfolk went out to get the buggies hitched.

The soldiers left as we did so, their truck disappearing quickly into the blinding rain. If anything, the wind was howling even more fiercely, and I was glad of the soldiers and their warning.

Nettie was even less eager to leave the barn, and there was a wild nervousness in her eyes as I coaxed and urged her out in the rain. I'd seen her spooked before, and I almost began to wish that I'd brought Pearl instead. After time at the plow, though, she needed her rest. Every creature needs their Sabbath.

Jacob and I hitched her up, and this time Jacob sat back with his mother and his sister as I drove Nettie homeward. She was struggling, I could feel it in her, but she kept on, as I muttered prayers under my breath. It was a harder ride back, though I'd not have thought that quite possible.

The wind snapped and shoved at the buggy, sometimes coming from one direction, sometimes from another. It knocked at the sides, and several of the gusts felt like they would almost knock us over, they were so fierce. Others caught the buggy from the front, and it buckled back on the leafsprings, and Nettie strained all the harder to pull us forward. Leaves and branches flew through the air.

In the back of the buggy, my little family clung to one another. Even Jacob, who had thought this all a great adventure, seemed less excited by the storm and more eager to get to our home.

In places, the water poured across the road, flowing deeper and deeper, splashing around Nettie's feet as if we were fording a stream. She has never liked water, and I wished even more that I had hitched up Pearl.

Once, and then again, I had to stop to move a fallen branch from the road, and by the second branch—which was quite large—even the parts of me that had been a little dry were soaked all the way through. Each time, it was harder to get Nettie going again.

Finally, she just stopped, about a mile from the house, as the driving rain and the howling and the intermittent peals of thunder became too much. I goaded and cajoled, but I could tell that she was terrified, and I have never been one to bring a whip too hard to bear on one of God's creatures.

It was not so cold, and I was already soaked to the skin, so I got out of the buggy, and went around to Nettie. She was wild-eyed under her blinders, nervous and barely containing herself. I petted her neck for a few moments, and talked to her for a little, my body in close against her head. Her breath came hot and tense against the wetness of my collar.

She calmed a little, I could tell. I took the reins and she followed behind me, pulling the buggy at my walking pace. It was hard to see, as the wind battered, but I just put one foot in front of another. My hat helped shelter my eyes, and it stayed on by some small miracle, but it has always been snug and perfect fitting.

It was a long mile.

We were glad to be home, when we finally arrived. Although I usually have Jacob stable Nettie, I had them go into the house, and I made sure she was in secure with Pearl before I made my way back.

IT IS STILL STORMING now, as I write here by candlelight. Dinner together was good, and although we were all a little disappointed that we did not have a chance to spend time with the Beilers and the other families, the pies were delicious.

We took a time for family prayer together after the meal, and all of us prayed for the storm to spare those who were not aware of its coming, and for those who are living near the sea. If it is like this here, it must be more terrible there.

The wind has grown all the stronger, and the house groans and creaks, and I can feel it shifting and moving slightly. Upstairs, water has been forced in past some of the windows, and Sadie and Jacob have been sopping it up with towels before the puddles on the floor spread too far.

Hannah and I spent much of our time after dinner in the dimly lit root cellar. It's by the barn, built into the earth to

keep it cool, and we use it for storage and for growing car-
rots and beets in the winter. But when the rain comes up,
the water weeps in, and while that is fine sometimes, this did
not look to be one of those times. By the light of a hurricane
lamp, with the storm shaking the door, she and I began to
move perishables higher on the shelving. Rice and grains must
be kept dry, and already the moisture was streaming in here
and there, pooling on the floor, as it does whenever we get a
long rain. We moved bags and boxes and containers to higher
shelves. It should be enough, and we can work to clear out
the water when the rain has stopped.

I checked again on the animals, as night fell, and they seem
to be doing all right. The cattle are tightly gathered under one
of the hay shelters, and they will weather the night accept-
ably. All of the other buildings on our little farm will manage.
The barn is a sturdy one, as is the unused *daadi haus*. And,
of course, the house itself. Where I am sitting, drying off yet
again. And where all of my little family are sitting, nestled
under blankets or reading.

On nights like this one, I am glad that the house was well
built. It had been one of the many houses owned by the
Schrock family, and some relative had lived here for many
years before it was put up for sale. I remember admiring the
craftsmanship of it when I came here to look for a place where
we could settle down in this community. It had been carefully constructed, the joists all doubly reinforced, the roof
secured against high wind, and insulation everywhere. It was

a good and sturdy home for the family we were sure we would have.

Still, it is not brick, and as it flexes and shifts, I am reminded that wood has limits, even if it is well used by careful hands. Everything in this world breaks, if you strain it hard enough.

October 12

It was a long night, and sleep did not come easily. When I awoke, the rain was still coming down in sheets, pouring down the side of the house, but the wind was dwindling away.

The barn seemed to have managed the night, as had the *daadi haus*. In the dull grayness of the morning, I could see branches down and scattered twigs and debris as I walked to feed the horses.

Sadie came with me, or rather, she ran ahead, as quickly as she could, covering her head with a shawl. Inside the barn, all was well, and though there was much moisture here and there, it looked like there was not much that needed to be repaired. I could see a bit of sky where the wind had pried some of the tin roof loose, but it hadn't fully pulled away. I would be able to repair it.

As we returned to the house, Jacob came running from the chicken coop, leaping puddles as he came up to us. He breathlessly announced that they were all fine.

My check of the larder showed that all was well, just a spot or two of moisture there. But when I went to the root cellar, opening that door revealed that it was not quite as fine as I would have hoped. Water stood to the height of my knees, a mess of muck that would have to be cleared out. But the work that Hannah and I did to move perishables was time well spent. I do not think we will lose anything.

It did not stop raining until early afternoon, and the wind rose on occasion, stirring and shaking the trees.

When the rain did take a break, I went to look at the work that I had done yesterday. It was a mess. Much of the soil had been washed away, and the seeds that we'd laid in had probably not fared much better. It was too soon for them to have sprouted, so maybe some would have survived, but whatever remained would not be neat and orderly. The Lord would give us patience, and we would deal with it in due time.

But there was not much about that I could attend to, because the immediate need was the cellar.

We moved the meat up into the house, where we hung it from the rafters in the kitchen. And then it was back down to the root cellar. I had a pair of waders, which years ago I had used for fishing. Wearing them, I went in, taking with me our three five-gallon buckets. For almost two hours we bailed, bucket after bucket, me to Hannah to Sadie to Jacob, who'd toss it and run it back. Over and over again, me to Hannah to Sadie to Jacob.

We sang a little bit as we worked, which made the business of clearing all that murky water not quite so terrible.

When the water level was low enough, the buckets were

joined by mops. I found myself remembering a movie I had seen on *rumspringa*, a cartoon with a mouse and magic, and the echo of the music from that film hummed in my head, just out of reach.

It would be nice to have such magic right now, I thought. But of course the whole point of that part of the movie was that you never know when the magic you rely on will overtake and drown you. It struck me as strangely like the magical world the English had made for themselves.

In the afternoon, the Jon Mail arrived, or at least that was what Sadie had taken to calling Jon's arrival on horseback.

Sadie came out to listen when she saw that he had arrived, and he tipped his hat to her. She just smiled.

And he smiled back, and cantered over toward her. There were words back and forth, nothings and trifles. Sadie's eyes flitted from the ground to Jon's face, back and forth, like a fisherman teasing a trout fly across the surface of a stream.

Jon seemed even more pleased, but as I was standing there, he remembered his purpose.

He asked if we were all okay, and if there was much help needed at our house. I told him no, that we were going to be fine, and then asked what news there was.

The community had weathered it well, he said. Some of the siding had been torn from the Thorsons' house, and another tree had fallen on their property, but it really hadn't been all that bad. There was damage to Deacon Sorenson's house, too, a big tear in the roof where the wind had caught it.

"Deacon Sorenson asked if you could come and help with

the repairs," Jon said. I told him that I could, once we'd dealt with things here around the house. Probably tomorrow, after I'd set in with the chores for the morning. I asked if Jon could ride and tell him, and he said he would. He said it with a smile, because he really and truly did love being Jon Mail.

I then asked him what else he heard, and if there was more news from the world. He had the news, of course.

After helping his family with the cleanup, Jon had ridden down to the Stauffers to see if there was any broader news about the storm.

There was a little, which had been conveyed by some soldiers who had passed the news from their radios. The storm had stayed mostly to the east of us, going north–northwest. There was a lot of flooding in Philadelphia, and some bridges had been washed out. From Lancaster and Lititz, the news was of many homes with flooded basements and damaged roofs. Many among the English needed sump pumps to keep their lower levels dry, and there was still no power to run them. With gas now scarce and functioning generators hard to come by, there was nothing to do but use mops and buckets.

"Not much other news," he said. "But there will be!" I knew he was right, of course.

As THE DAY TURNED to dusk and darkness, I spent some time sorting through my tools and preparing what I will need to bring to the Sorensons' tomorrow. In one of the drawers of my workbench, as I was gathering up the nails I would need, I found myself for a moment contemplating my pistol. It sat there, black as night, in the drawer in my work-room where I keep it.

It is a Smith & Wesson revolver, an old Model 29 with a four-inch barrel, and a well-worn wood handle. I have had it for many years, a gift from my father. I took it out and I cleaned it, inspecting the action. I checked the boxes of ammunition, mostly .44 Magnum. It kicks like a mule, but the more powerful load makes it more useful. It is a simple thing, a simple tool, and I use it for slaughtering cattle. It is quick. It gets the job done. My father also had another gun, a rifle, which he used occasionally for slaughter, but mostly for hunting. In this settlement, they are a little less common, but most of the men I know own one. Isaak does not, and Deacon Sorenson does not, because they choose not to. But for many of us, particularly those with livestock, it was just something that we needed.

As I will need it, next week, for that steer, which is why it was good to check it now. I cleaned it, carefully, as I do regularly. Tools must be maintained.

I know that among the English, there are many guns. Like the guns that the soldiers carry, weapons kept in preparation for use against neighbors or strangers. They keep them in their drawers at their bedsides, or in cabinets, and the feel of their ownership of guns is very different. It is a feeling of pride. A feeling of power.

It seems to me that it is all based on a feeling of fear. To keep a gun because you are afraid of dying, and because you want to be ready to kill another human being, it just feels like such a strange thing. So filled with pride, and so dead to God. I do not understand it. Why would I fear dying, when we all die?

I do fear God, and God's just judgment on sinners. Jesus taught us that we should never allow the world's hate to move our hands against others among God's children. I know these things as if they are written into me.

Holding it in my hands, feeling the heft and weight and purpose of that object, I found my mind turning to Tom and to that stranger whose body was abandoned by the side of the road. And to the men we now see, our English neighbors, carrying their guns openly by the roadside.

I think that is why Tom had so many guns, past any possible need. For some, I think, they are just toys, like some among the English collect cars or clothes. But for him, it was different. He lived in fear, fear of failing, fear of the world he was living in. And having those guns made him feel strong, and made him feel safe, even though those objects could not feed his children or make his heart less angry. Maybe it was like the alcohol that way.

I know that whoever killed that man left by the side of the road probably held their guns for the same reason. I wonder what they felt, as they killed him. Did they feel as I feel, when I put down a pig or a cow? That is easy to do, because I know why I must do it.

I do not hate a cow. It simply is, and I must kill it if I am to eat and feed my family. I take its life, but I am thankful for it. That animal is part of God's Providence for me and my family, and I remember to be grateful, as I am grateful for the fields and the harvest.

When we kill another person, something must be broken in us. We have forgotten who they are, and have forgotten who we are. How could they see that person as a child of God, loved by God as they are loved?

I could not imagine it. It is the strangest thing about the English, the thing that is beyond me.

I set the gun away, and remembered that I would need to sharpen the blades, too, if I am going to slaughter the steer this week.

October 15

It has been a very busy few days, so much so that I did not have time to write.

Tuesday I went to the Sorensons', and spent much of the day working on the damage to their roof. The storm had done far more damage than I would have thought. It had torn away shingles and a large section of subroofing near the front of the house, by winds that had been much stronger than the ones that we encountered. Just a few miles away.

But storms can be strange that way, leaving one house untouched and shattering another. It is just the way of Creation. And as the story of Job teaches us, it is not a sign that a man or a family is sinful or that they've turned from God. It is just that we are humble, small creatures, and the vastness of God's creation can break us so easily.

And it breaks our houses. The work took much of the morning and early afternoon. I did not have a chance to bring anything by for the pickup of supplies at the Schrocks' house, but I did see the trucks moving off. I wondered who went with them this time, then learned the next day when Young Jon came riding by that the mess in Lancaster was bad, because so many people had the lower levels of their houses flooded. This was especially true in a couple of new neighborhoods on the outer edge of town, where the big houses were all stacked up next to each other. Huge houses, they all were, with room enough for a family of seven or eight, but most with just two or three people in them.

I went inside one, once, a couple of years ago, to install some custom cabinetry. It was a project that Mike had helped set up. The house was immense, bigger than a barn, and decorated like a palace. The people who lived there were really nice people, a pleasant older couple who had moved to Lancaster to retire. But the house was so big for them. Downstairs, they had a theater and an exercise room and a study and a bar. I thought about the *daadi haus*, built for parents, which could have fit twice over on just one of their three levels.

So much more than needed, I thought. But I did not say it, because that would have been rude, and they were a kind couple.

Those big homes all had big basements, and now most were badly flooded.

Out front of many of the homes, there were now piles of sodden furniture and torn-out carpeting, stained with mud and clay. Those had joined with the piles of trash that had been accumulating for some time, as trash collection simply could not happen. Most of the trucks were not operating, and even if they had been, the military had requisitioned whatever fuel might be available.

Jon said that there were many, many more people at the market distribution site today. Even the well prepared, those who were ready with several weeks of emergency supplies, even they were beginning to run low.

There was more anxiety, and more impatience, and less food. They have cut back on what they are giving out, because the first line of supplies, "those kept ready for an emergency," are beginning to run out. One angry man began shouting when he was stopped from taking more than his share. The guardsmen tried to send him off, but he punched a market volunteer, and then tried to take one of the guards' rifles, and so they subdued and arrested him and then took him off somewhere.

"It really is getting worse," Jon said. "On the ride back, I heard that there was a big firefight between police and National Guard and some armed gangs from Philadelphia. Not like street gangs, these were just armed men who had gathered together to take what they needed. The gangs had moved from looting stores to moving through neighborhoods, taking food from every house, and shooting anyone who wouldn't give them what they wanted.

"Some had made it to Norristown, and there a neighborhood militia had begun fighting back, and then the Guard arrived, and many were killed. So many desperate people, and not enough food. The sergeant who gave me a ride back told me that they are talking about not just closing the highways, but shutting down the borders of the state. People aren't just fighting inside the cities. Many are starting to leave, he hears. Thousands of them, hungry and carrying what they can, moving out toward the countryside, especially in the south. Everyone, fleeing the city, coming out to where they think they might be able to find something to eat."

It was terrible news, but it did not surprise me.

IT IS STRANGE, TO live in a time like this, when things feel so dangerous. But things have been very hard in the past, too. Every day, every day since I have been here in this settlement, I read from the *Martyrs Mirror*. That old book was a favorite of my father and especially my uncle, who, when he preached, would refer again and again to the sufferings of the martyrs throughout the ages. When I was a young man, the taste of the book had grown bitter in my mouth.

Yet when I came here, and in a time of testing and prayer Jonas Beiler heard of my spiritual struggle, it was he who told me to set aside that bitterness. Do not let the poison of your spirit keep you from the truth. Do not forget the power of a time of testing.

And so as I write, every day, I remember. Writing the words helps me remember.

All of those stories—of the martyrs, of faith in the crucible of suffering, of how good Christians have experienced and endured times of terrible torture and privation—I remember thinking to myself, so often, about how far away all of those things seemed. Here we were, and we prospered. Our hard work and diligence was rewarded by Providence. There was food, there was plenty, and our faith was without trial. It was easy to become prideful, or to become convinced of God's protection.

Yes, we had to be disciplined, and yes, being among our brethren and renouncing the easy path of the English required strength of purpose. But the kind of strength to endure times of trial, and to stand unwilling to turn a hand against those who would harm us? Would starve us? Would destroy our bodies, even as our souls remain intact? That, for a while, has been a trial that we have not had to endure in this country.

Now, though, the time has shifted. The world itself has shifted. I must trust in my faith, that it will endure this testing.

Is that not the purpose of faith? Surely it is.

I PREPARE TO MAKE more jerky. I think I will do so on Saturday. Today I inspected the drying houses and found that my newest one had been a little beaten up in the storm. One of the side windows had been smashed, which is fixable. I will need to get replacement glass, or perhaps even just clear plastic. I would prefer to stay with glass, as it does not need to be insulated and there is much old single-pane to be had still. I do not think this will be a problem. In fact, I am sure I know where to get it.

As I thought about the drying houses, I found myself flipping back through my last journal, to the beginning, to remember something. It was when I built this last of the houses that I had tried to persuade Bishop Schrock to let me build something new.

I found the entries, from July and August one year ago.

· I wanted to try a new design, one I'd seen in other settlements, after I had built the passive radiator houses. It was a tunnel dryer, one that heated air across a long chamber, which was then force-fed into the drying house by a solar-powered fan array.

It dried much faster, and in larger quantities, and I was eager to find a way to expand my business. I could see four or five of them, and maybe expanding so that selling dried meat could become my main business. Carpentry was so inconsistent, as useful as it was, and it felt like the right thing to do to ensure that our household had income.

But Bishop Schrock had balked. He felt it seemed unnecessarily complex, more potentially prideful. He told me I needed to pray over it, and to set such thoughts aside for a while.

Back then, I really did not quite grasp why he felt this way. Other communities in nearby districts used the same method, I argued, ones that we are in fellowship with. I did not see why I should not do the same.

We have already allowed one solar array, he had said. We do not yet know how that array will test us, or if it will be something the Order can make a larger part of our path.

And so he had told me that I should not put in the tunnel dryers, that I needed to wait.

I remember feeling that this might not be fair, and that to wait did not make sense. Yet I did, and instead of building a tunnel dryer, I built another passive panel dryer.

And now I am glad that it happened as it did. If I had built those dryers, they would not work now. The solar storm had shorted out the one array that existed in the settlement, in a way that could not be repaired.

And so now, instead of being down one drying house, I have all three working. Strange how Providence can work, with hardship proving to be the thing that strengthens us.

I MARVEL, THIS EVENING, at Sadie. She is still a slender and flighty bird, a delicate thing. But her change over these last few weeks has been a miracle, the kind of change that Hannah and I had been praying for since first she had her seizures. There have been none, not since the Blackout began. I do not know how that can be.

She seems more at ease, and it is as if the tension has flown from her face. It is fuller, softer, younger. When she speaks, in passing or to her mother, I can hear a difference. Or I think I can.

I am thankful, certainly. It is a blessing.

October 16

This afternoon, Mike arrived again. I had been wondering about him, and praying over him, and worrying over him. It had been long since I saw him, as I had not been able to see him when I went to Lancaster.

And then, as I was finishing up some repair work to one of the meat dryers, there he was. He came trudging up the drive, pushing that bicycle, behind which was a makeshift trailer. He was not alone.

Behind him, just a few strides back, were his two sons, Derek and Tad, sixteen and fourteen, each with a large pack, each pulling a wagon filled with supplies. One, a child's red wagon, the other, a two-wheeled lawn cart. And behind them, a woman I knew from a picture I had seen once.

Shauna, his ex-wife. She was a little older, and quite a bit heavier than in the picture, but it was her.

"Jacob," he said.

"Mike," I said, and moved forward to greet him. We shook hands, and he introduced me to his sons. Derek was broad and heavy, a big man like his father, and he mumbled as he greeted me. Tad was long and lean, and he smiled broadly but said nothing.

And then he introduced me to Shauna, who smiled tentatively and told me she was glad to finally meet me.

Mike put an arm around my shoulder, as he did whenever he was trying to talk me into something, and said, "Jacob, can we go talk?"

I told him sure, that of course we could, and told him that the boys and Shauna should go to the house and sit for a while.

So we walked toward the barn, and as we walked he talked to me about how things had been. He was always a persuasive talker, a good salesman, but now his sales pitch seemed frail. And he seemed frail, I thought, as I looked at him. Thinner than I'd seen him before.

"You walked all of this way?" I asked.

"Yeah," he said. "Started out at, like, ten. About five hours. Man, I miss my truck."

We were silent for a minute. It seemed pointless to speak in pleasantries. Then he broke the silence.

"I'm running out of food," he said. "You know I was ready, you know how much I kept, all those supplies."

I told him that I did, because he was always talking about how important it was to be prepared for emergencies. Usually that subject would come with him talking about how people were irresponsible and lazy, about how they just relied on the government for everything. He did not say that today, and I did not mention it.

"Since that storm, things are just getting worse, and I don't know how much longer we can make it. There's not enough food coming in on the trucks now, and we all know it, like everybody knows it, and there isn't any way to get food, and I'm worried. Three of my neighbors had their homes busted into the last two days. Three. And one time, there was shooting. I mean, right there, three houses down, middle of the night. *Bam bam bam.* A couple of guys from the neighborhood, part of the new watch, they got shot. The thieves took off, I think they killed one of them."

He seemed sheepish, a little off, not the usual Mike who was always filled with bluster and self-certainty. His eyes were tired, a little hollow. "And it isn't just that it's not safe. I can't stay at my place anymore. There's roof damage, and it's leaking, and the whole lower level of the townhouse still has three feet of water in it. It smells like rot and mildew, and Tad started having trouble breathing. You know his asthma, how that's always been hard for him. And we're running out of asthma medication."

I asked him how we could help, even though I already knew why he was there, and I knew the answer.

"I know it's a ton to ask. I know it. But can we stay awhile with you? We don't need much, really we don't. And you have that place out back, you know, where you store stuff. We wouldn't get in the way. The boys and I can help out around the place, we really can. And Shauna . . . well . . . shoot . . . yeah."

I asked about that, because they really never could get along.

"But you know, Shauna, she's the mother of my kids. She's their mom. When I told the boys about the idea of maybe coming out here, they were, like, what about Mom? I mean, she's their mom. And, she's, like, got nobody. Yeah, some friends, but they were kind of a mess before this all started. I can't just leave her in town all by herself. That'd be . . . well . . . I couldn't do that."

We went back and forth for a little bit after that, but I knew that I couldn't send him away. I told him to wait on the porch. Then I went to talk with Hannah, who was working in the garden, replanting and trying to restore it after the damage from the storm.

She took it really very well. But what choice did we have? Here, on our doorstep, neighbors in need. Even if they had been strangers coming to our door, asking for help, what would we have done? It really was very simple, deciding that we would put them up.

She and Sadie went with Shauna and the boys to help get the *daadi haus* set up. It was two small rooms, a small bath to wash, and a storage area upstairs. A little woodburning stove for heat. And that was it. There was one bed, but there was also an old sofa, and we had a spare mattress that I kept in the storage area.

I asked him about his girlfriend, Jolie. Wasn't she pregnant? Where was she?

"Yeah, well," he said. "Now I don't think it was mine. I did, but then she and this other guy took off, went down south with someone who had a truck, before all the roads got closed. I think it was his kid. I don't know where she got off to. Can't really care right now. I mean, it's her life, right?"

I said that it was sad, and he agreed with me.

We talked a little more about what he could do, and how he and the boys and Shauna might be able to help out.

AFTER DINNER, AFTER READING and a time for family prayers, our guests went to the *daadi haus* to settle in for the night. Hannah and I curled up in bed, lying face to face as we talked.

It is an old habit, and it feels good. Warm and gentle and safe. It reminds me of when we bed dated. She did not want to sleep.

"Jay," she said, "you know this will make everything harder."

I said that I did.

"You know that feeding four more mouths will push what we can do here as a family. And I know they want to help, but I don't know how ready they are to do what they will need to do to keep us afloat."

I said that I knew it, and asked her if she thought we could do any different.

She sighed. "No. No we can't. In the Bible, Abram and Sarah didn't turn aside the angels who walked their way. And the widow, she didn't turn out Elijah, even in her time of hardship. This is what the Lord has put on us, and we must receive it and let our lives bear witness."

I told her that I was thinking the same things, and about what Jesus had said about walking the extra mile, and giving even more than what is asked. Then I said that this was what martyr really meant. "Witness." I had learned that from someone, years ago. That the word just meant *witness*. Sometimes being a witness is easier, I said, quietly. You can be true to the Gospel, and live your life so that every word and deed is Gospel. The world will nod and smile, and say what a nice person you are, and all will be simple. But sometimes it's really hard, and being a witness can mean terrible things.

This would be a hard time.

"Yes," she said. "I know it. And for me, it is easy. I know what we must face. For you, it is easy. But I wish it did not have to be so for Sadie and Jacob. What a mother and father can endure, they would still not wish on their children. Oh, Jay."

We held each other for a while.

Then she fell asleep. I did not, not for a while. But now I am tired. Writing does that.

October 17

In the morning, I woke with the sunrise. I got the feed in for the cows, and Jacob fed the chickens, and Sadie and Hannah worked to prepare the breakfast.

Mike had said that he would be helping me in the morning, and I will confess that I was a little surprised to see him and Tad and Derek all waiting by the kitchen door. They all looked tired, but Mike asked me what they could do.

First, of course, was breakfast. I asked if Shauna would be joining us, but Mike said she was feeling out of sorts and tired, and couldn't get out of bed.

"Oh dear Lord God you have coffee" was the first thing Mike said as they came with me into the kitchen and smelled what was being prepared. It was like one long word, *ohdearlordgodyouhavecoffee*, and though he apologized, I thought it was a little funny.

Out at one of the tree stands on the edge of the property, an old oak had fallen during the storm, and it laid out into one of the pastures. It had broken the fence, and I had not yet been able to get around to repairing it. It was a task that required many hands, and with all of the damage done by the storm, it was not yet a priority. I was not worried about losing a few head of cattle, because the tree itself stood as an effective barrier to their departure.

So with the day still young, I asked Mike and his boys to take lumber from the barn, to saw up the tree and chop it for firewood, and fix the fence. He nodded, and Tad smiled, and Derek grunted sleepily.

We worked much of the morning. Mike is so handy, and a good man to work by your side. Work lights him up, and he delights in it.

Tad and Derek are . . . well . . . they are still young. They will learn, as they stay here.

IT WAS NOT TERRIBLE, having Mike and his boys here today. With no family here, with such a small household, I feel often as if we are a burden on the others. It is not a good feeling, and it is not a feeling that is right.

I know that we are all called to support and bless one another with care. It is a simple truth, that we all serve one another. I know it. And I have been told, again and again over the ten years that we have been here, that we are a blessing to this community. But I still harbor an old anger. I pray over it, and it disperses, as the Spirit gives the grace, but I know it will return.

I felt a twinge of it today, as we all sat at table. It was a simple dinner, and a good one, which Shauna had helped prepare, once she had woken. Hannah told me today that they talked, Shauna and Sadie and her, and that Shauna began to feel more at ease. The last two weeks had frightened her, and she had always struggled with fear and anxiety.

She seems to have pulled herself together a bit. Hannah is good for that.

And so the dinner was prepared, canned beef stew and winter squash, kale from the garden, bread and jam, simple and enough.

Around the table, there was talk and some laughter, and the house felt full. Still, I felt the stirring of something dark afterward.

I think it is an anger from our time of leaving, when I finally realized that we could no longer stay in the Ohio settlement founded by my uncle. We knew it was coming, but it was still hard, because both Hannah and I had been raised among those people.

So many were our friends, not just our family, and our bonds went far back. But after Sarah died in the womb, and after we learned that we would not be having more children, things changed. It was whispered among the women that this was judgment for pridefulness, and Hannah was deeply hurt.

When the whispering continued, month after month, I had brought it to my uncle, and he seemed to only affirm it. He said I needed to examine my heart for sin. I needed to consider why God had inflicted this punishment on my family, and to repent of it.

When I was a child, not yet a man, I would have yielded

to this judgment. Submission and humility are how all must live, and accepting the authority of those chosen to lead is part of that. But I knew enough of the world, not the English world, but of other settlements and other districts. I had been through the wandering-around, and it had taken me places where things were different.

I knew the anger that such broken instruction stirred in me was righteous, and biblical. Job did not suffer because of sin. Christ did not suffer because he was sinful, and neither did the martyrs and the apostles. Good men were not punished by sickness, and good women did not suffer because they deserved it.

To say otherwise felt like a failure to grasp why our Lord and Savior had lived and died.

It felt like *hochmut*, like sinful pride at work in those who prospered. I felt it strongly, though I am not as strong in the spirit as my wife. It became a powerful wedge, driven between my uncle and me like an adz bites into dry wood. I prayed over it, and I prayed over it, but it would not leave.

I began to realize that my anger at it was not pride, but the thing that stirred me and made me determined to stand firm. It was not an anger that strikes a blow, or speaks a word of hatred. I was never disrespectful. It was, instead, the anger that tells you that a wound has been inflicted.

It was for that reason most of all that we left. Why I sold off all of the holdings and property that had been given me, and sought land in a settlement where there was more grace. It was a miracle that I found this house at just a time when land prices here were falling to within reach. Coming here proved so much easier than I had thought.

I only wish anger was as easy to leave behind.

I will pray over this more. But still, it is good to have the house filled with sound and with life.

October 18

This Sabbath day was to be a day of prayer, as it is every other week in normal times. I had told Mike and Shauna that yesterday. There were the very basic chores to accomplish, as there always were. But for the morning, the four of us would gather for a time of readings and praying, and sometimes we would sing. I wanted our guests to know that this was not our being inhospitable, and they told us that they understood.

I think Mike and the boys were really tired from all that they'd done the day before, so Mike said they would probably sleep in. Shauna, though, asked if she could sit with us, as we prayed and as we read together, and Hannah told her that it would be fine.

They had talked about it much yesterday, and so there she was, with us.

We sat in silence. It did not seem, this day, like we should try to sing together as a family from the *Ausbund* as we sometimes do. It would not be welcoming to Shauna, because she does not know the language, and so instead we shared readings from the Psalms in English.

When it came time to talk, our family custom was that I would say a few words about a scripture, and then Hannah, and then Sadie, and then Jacob. That is the blessing of a shared family worship, this time of reflection. So we each chose and read a passage.

I chose to read from Job, because that was where God has been leading me these last weeks. We read in English, because again it would not be right to have a guest with us and not to let her join us.

I do not know how Bishop Schrock would feel about this, but I know that it was what we needed to do.

Hannah read from the twenty-third Psalm, where she so often goes for comfort, and then shared her trust in God in a short reflection. Sadie chose to read a passage from Luke, one that talks about the coming of the Kingdom and the end of things, and how it is already among us. It was that passage I'd been reflecting on the other day, about the vultures gathering over a corpse.

"I think we all know what that means," Sadie said, as she closed the Bible and passed it to her brother. And that was all she had to say about that.

Jacob read from 1 Samuel, as he often does, the story of David and Goliath. He reads it because he likes it. Because it makes him feel brave, even though he's not grown up. That was what he said.

"I'm very scared when I look out at the English now. I still dream about those planes falling down, about the fires, and I feel small and like I am nothing. But then I remember how David was strong, even though he was just a kid. Especially because he was a kid. He was smart and fast, and he knew what to do. So I like this story right now."

When the Bible was passed to Shauna, she read from the Psalms again, a little passage from Psalm 51, about creating in her a clean heart.

And then she talked, and she cried, and she talked some more. About how afraid and alone she felt. About how she had already been so lonely and isolated, because of how things had been. She had always been anxious, and afraid, and she had turned to alcohol and men who were not her husband. She had lost her job as a nurse's assistant at the hospital because she had let her life slide, and had done things she should not have done. She had not known how to talk to her boys when they became teenagers, and they had hated her because she had done terrible things and been a terrible mom.

Then she cried for a while, and Hannah and Sadie held her, and she said she was sorry for crying, and then she cried some more.

Then we prayed from the prayer book to end our family time, as we always do.

I think it was good that she could be with us. The lives of the English are so very hard.

THAT AFTERNOON, WE DID not work, for it was Sabbath. Sadie and Hannah went with Shauna, Tad, and Derek to visit at the Fishers'. I would go later, but for now, I stayed with Mike, and he and I talked and walked the property along the fence line. There were things we needed to discuss.

There were things he needed to hear from me.

"From what you have told me, and what I have seen, you are not going to be weekend guests, Mike. This is going to last a while, maybe a very long while."

He nodded, grimly. "Yeah. I don't know how this turns out. I can't see it being good."

I told him about what we would be able to do for the winter, which would be on us soon. There was harvesting that needed to happen yet. Soon it would be the wheat that had survived the storm, the root vegetables that still grew deep in the earth, the fall crop.

And with four more mouths, our preparations were barely adequate. I'd need to slaughter that calf, soon, tomorrow, and he and the boys could help me butcher it and prepare it. That meat would help.

But it would mean less for us to give when others came hungry to us. It would mean that we would need to keep a positive spirit toward one another, and the work would be hard.

I asked him if he was willing to commit to doing what needed to be done.

"We've worked together so long, Jacob," he said. "You know I'm good for doing whatever we gotta do to make this happen. And do I have a choice? I mean seriously, do I?"

I told him that I knew I could trust him, but that sometimes what we mean to do and what we do become very different things.

"Yeah," he said. "I hear that. Story of my life."

Then I told him that we needed to talk about Shauna. Would they be able to be together and not be angry? "It is going to be a very hard time, no matter what happens," I said. "If we work together, and are careful, and make sure that we spend ourselves not on anger and tearing each other down but on building up, then God will reward us as God sees fit.

"If we do not, then . . ."

"Yeah, I know," he said. "Too much drama. Too much drama. Can't do the drama if we want to survive."

"Can you stay away from it?" I asked him. "There has been so much bitterness the two of you have shared. And she still hurts from it, as do you."

"I'll try," he said. I could tell that he meant it.

Then we talked about how to slaughter a steer, because it helps to be prepared to do something like that.

THE AFTERNOON AT THE Fishers' was good. Mike chose to stay at our place, said he needed to think about some things. After the meal, we shared a dessert of Rachel's bread pudding. It was graham crackers and whipped cream and sugar, mixed together with a pudding mix, so it was not really and actually bread pudding as I remembered it from my childhood.

But it was very delicious. "How do you eat this and stay so thin?" I heard Shauna say.

Joseph and I talked together for a while about what we were hearing these last few days.

News was worsening from everywhere. More and more hungry people, and people without enough. More angry people, more stories of violence and death.

Even the soldiers seemed to be struggling with it. He had heard from Bill, who had talked with someone in Lititz, that some Guardsmen were beginning to return to their homes, because they were afraid for their families and children. Bill said he didn't see the difference himself, but that others had told him that there were fewer police and soldiers.

Maybe it was just a rumor.

What could be seen was that more men were on the streets with guns, and there were not one but three militias and neighborhood protection groups just in the area. Bill himself was part of one, one made up of farmers and local business-men who wanted to be sure that no one took advantage of their crops, or raided their homes at night.

"Is there any good news?" I asked. "Surely there must be something good."

He thought for a minute or two. "One of the bigger English farms on the other side of the county had gotten a couple of their combines running now," said Joseph. "They fixed them up with parts from other things. Finding gas isn't easy, but it has helped. The wheat they've harvested has gone to a couple of bakeries in Lancaster, where they've figured out a way to get the ovens going again. That means bread, which is something that everyone is happy about. Even if it isn't quite enough."

I agreed that was good, and hoped we'd see more of it soon.

Joseph nodded, and there was a pause as we watched those around us, the children running and playing, the women sitting, talking. It was like it had been last month, six months ago, a year ago. As if nothing had happened. Nothing for a hundred years.

It was a moment of forgetting. Sometimes, forgetting is God's most gracious blessing.

October 19

The wind rose up this morning, blowing hard from the north, bringing clouds that were high and swift and stark. It was colder again, and the sharp winds bore a bite in them that was not there yesterday.

It was a good day for slaughter. Too hot makes it feel messier, and there is the risk of the meat spoiling quickly. But with the temperature suddenly below fifty, it is almost like we have been blessed with refrigeration. The Lord is good in His Providence.

After breakfast, Mike joined me as we retrieved the steer from the field. We led it toward the area behind the shed. The rest of the herd was a far way off, and the young bull did not fight or make it difficult. They almost never do.

Why would it? Being fed was the most likely thing to expect, and I am never cruel with them, so they have no cause to fear me.

I had sent Jacob and Derek to get the blades and the pistol, and they returned, Derek carrying the various different blades in their leather pouch, and Jacob carrying the pistol and a box of ammunition. Tad was not with us. He had heard that we were going to be killing the steer, and decided that he'd rather help his mother and Hannah and Sadie with the cleaning up after breakfast, and to prepare for making the large batch of beef stew.

"That's gonna be nasty," he said, and that was his reason. I notice, however, that he has been making an effort to talk with Sadie and that may be another reason. A father does not miss such things.

As Jacob handed me the Smith & Wesson, Derek looked at the old revolver with fascination. "I didn't know Amish people had guns," he said. "My dad taught me to shoot at the range and all, but I thought you didn't ever have that sort of thing. You know, because you're so . . . I don't know. You just can't hurt people, right?"

I loaded one of the fat rounds into the chamber of the pistol. "We have knives, too," I said with a smile. "But they are tools for farmers and hunters. Nothing more. Harming another to protect ourselves would betray what we believe. That would be pride, and it would be killing, and it would not be what Jesus taught us."

He nodded.

I asked him if he had ever seen an animal killed, and he said that he hadn't.

I led the steer to a post near the barn, right by the hitch we would use to lift the carcass, and secured it lightly. Then I set a bucket of feed in front of it. It began to eat, head down. I stepped forward, and as I did so, Jacob plugged his ears, and Derek and Mike did the same. I put the round cleanly into the animal's forehead. It fell sideways, then rolled over on its side, legs twitching, straight out in front of it.

Such a kick, that pistol has. I can still feel it in my hand, even as I write this.

A smaller caliber rifle would work as well, and be more practical. Especially for hunting. But this was a gift, and one should use a gift, especially one that is so practical. And the truth is I rarely hunt.

I asked Jacob for the curved blade, and he handed it to me, still sharp. I cut into the throat, and blood fountained out, the scent of it filling the air. It is an old pattern, so familiar.

Mike seemed to take it in stride. He was a soldier, for a while. But Derek? His large, ruddy face lost some of its normal color. He looked a little pale and dizzy.

He remained pale for a while, but he stayed with us the whole time, as we hoisted the steer and bled it and skinned it and gutted it and prepared the cuts. I will admit I was impressed. I do not think that I did that well the first time I helped my father.

I told him so, and he seemed pleased.

WELL BEFORE THE DAY was over, we had finished with the butchering. It was not quite as much meat as I had hoped, because the forage and the feed have not been as good in the pastures. But it was still close to five hundred pounds of beef.

Jacob is a quick hand with the blade, as he has learned much from me over the last few years.

Mike and Derek mostly helped with the cleanup and simpler preparation, like cutting the meat and preparing it for curing, or bringing it to the house, where every pot was turned to making the stew for canning and storage.

The house hummed with working together, all eight of us turned to the same purpose, and I felt good of it.

The day went swiftly by, as a day blessed with productive work does, like a song or a heartfelt prayer.

And the steaks at dinner were delicious.

TONIGHT AS I PRAYED, I found myself giving thanks for Mike and his family, for the speed with which they worked and were willing to learn. I would not have thought it, if I am honest with myself.

A part of my soul would have assumed, as would many of those in the settlement, that those who live among the English and are part of them just cannot bring themselves to work as we do. That is part of the greatest danger to our souls, a pride that can come when we set ourselves apart to be servants, but then assume that our servanthood makes us better.

Bishop Beiler would talk about that all of the time. It was in the first sermon I heard from him, when I came here to get a sense of this settlement, in the time of parting. It was his last sermon to us, in those days before the cancer took him. If we look at our simple way, and let ourselves become proud of it, then *demut* becomes *hochmut*. Our strength becomes our downfall. That is how Satan works in all of us, tearing us from God's love.

It is like the bitter heart of the elder brother of the prodigal, sitting resentful in the field. Or the resentments of the laborers, when even the latecomers to the field are given wages from the generosity of their employer. Jesus knew our hearts, so easily turned to pride and hate.

But Mike and his family can be a blessing to us. And we to them, if we keep ourselves turned to the task of blessing one another.

GUNFIRE HAS WOKEN ME again. It crackles and pops, far distant. It has lasted for a while. I cannot sleep for worrying.

October 20

It was colder still this morning, and a light frost lay on the ground from the night before. But the day was beginning clear, and I was thankful for that, as bright sun was needed these next few days.

This afternoon, we would be ready to fill all three of the drying houses with the cured meat, and I checked the houses. All were cleaned and ready. As I rested my hand against the clear side of one, I felt the warmth of the rising sun already heating the space within.

But before that, there were other things to do.

Tuesday was here again, and we had set aside a case of stew for giving, and some of the cabbage from the garden, which I would take to the Schrock farm once the morning's tasks were done.

Before I left, Jon arrived with news. It was about the gunfire last night. A dozen armed looters had tried to break in to the Stauffers, though there was almost nothing left on the shelves. They had smashed the windows and tried to take whatever they could get their hands on.

There had been a firefight between the looters and some of the men from the town. It lasted for a while, and ranged nearby as they pursued the men. Five or six were dead.

And then Jon handed me a handwritten message, one from Bishop Schrock. After all of the food had been loaded onto the National Guard trucks to be taken to market, he would like to talk with me. I knew what our conversation would be about.

Like the rising of the sun or the phases of the moon, I thought.

Again, about Mike.

Jon knew what it was about, too. I suppose everyone did, as everyone always knows everything. It would be the same conversation we had many times.

But now it would be different, I knew. So much was different now. I sighed, and said a little prayer.

I ARRIVED AT THE farm, and helped with the loading. Two trucks today.

Bishop Schrock asked me to walk with him along the fence that bordered his pastures. It could have been a very long walk, because the Schrock farm is the largest in the settlement.

We talked for a short while about the labor of the farm, about the change in the weather, about the coming of the cold. And then, as I knew it would, the conversation turned to my guests.

"You know what I have told you about the dangers of being too close to Englishers like your friend," he said. "His life is broken."

I told him that I remembered our conversations, yes.

"And now he has come to live with you, with his children and a woman to whom he is no longer married."

I told him that was so.

Bishop Schrock stopped walking, and looked out into his fields. His face seemed tight, his eyes not on mine.

"I never thought I would see this time, Jacob. A terrible time, a time of trial and testing."

I did not say anything, because I was not sure quite what he meant.

He went on. "I do what I can to watch out for our spiritual integrity. The ways of the world can so easily destroy us, and work their way into our souls. The English are all around us, and our path is all we have that gives us strength. I know I can be hard. But that is needed, if we are to serve God."

His eyes turned to me. "I hope you know this. I only do what I do because I must. It is my duty."

I told him yes, and though my voice was calm, my heart was not. It stirred, leapt, and I could feel that old anger rising. Those words were my father's words, and my uncle's words. Those very words.

He looked away again, out to his fields. He was silent for another moment, his eyes far away.

"You must continue to let your friend and his family live with you."

"What!" I said. It squeezed out of me on a breath, like I was a crumpled paper bag. "What?"

He did not look at me, but he spoke plainly.

"You must let him stay with you. And the woman who was his wife, and his children. These are not times like other times, Jacob. Around us, the English are dying. They are dying. We give our food, and we give our skills, but we are so few, Jacob. Whenever the soldiers come, I hear things that tell me this. Every time, and it worsens. There will be so many terrible days ahead.

"I know I have told you to be wary, to be careful around Mike. And when I heard that he had come to you, I was troubled. But I have prayed, and prayed with Liza. She is a good woman, as is your Hannah. She bears grace in her more deeply than I, and reminded me of what Jonas Beiler would have done. Prayers do not always give us the answers we assumed we would get."

His mouth worked a little bit, as it always did when he struggled with something.

"I . . . am not Jonas Beiler. I have never been him. I did not choose this, to be Bishop. I did not want it when it was given to me. It all came easily for Jonas, even the hard things. Because of his simple kindness and wisdom, the families came, as you did. More of the young stayed. His every word seemed to be grace. I am . . . not so good at that. I am clumsy at it. I feel like a child learning to milk a cow. But I try. We were different, I know, but he was my friend. I wish he were here now."

There was silence. I still did not know what to say. He went on.

"And in this time, as everything we know falls apart, all we have to hold on to is our way. But what is our simple way, and all of our actions, if we cannot welcome the hungry? And be hospitable to the homeless stranger in our land? It is our burden. It is a sacrifice. It is a duty. Even if it destroys our bodies, or brings us hunger. We have no choice, but to be as Christ taught."

I nodded.

We stood there for a few more moments, and then he turned back toward the farmhouse.

"Come. Have some coffee," he said.

THE DAY HAD GROWN cloudy by the afternoon, so the meat will cure for another half-day. That will be fine. It will only add flavor.

MY HEART FEELS STRANGE tonight. I thought about this during my evening prayers. It is hard to explain. It feels like something has broken in me, but in a good way. Like a band of steel in my chest was cut, and suddenly I am a little more alive. I had become so used to it that I didn't even realize it was there anymore. And now it is gone, and I feel different. I feel fuller, stronger, released.

I did not know how much anger I must have been carrying in me. It is that same anger, from being driven from a place that I had called my home. I know I had carried it here, as we carry our demons with us wherever we go.

And then the Spirit had moved in Asa Schrock, and it had broken something in him, which broke something in me. I have never seen him as he is, I think. Always "Bishop." Always seeing him as the role, and not seeing him as a brother. And when I think of him as "Bishop," I am seeing the image of "Bishop" I had in my head. I brought that image with me, as a hard, cold idol carried in my soul. I did not let that idol stand between me and Jonas, because Jonas was so different. But Asa? I could not see him. I only saw echoes of my uncle. And my father.

I feel so filled with gratitude for this day. As hard as this time is and will be, I am still grateful.

October 21

The news of the morning was that the delivery in Lancaster had not gone well. Again, there were disruptions, and the crowd was bigger, and there was less food. People were hungrier, and women were crying, and men were angry and most were armed. Order was maintained, but everyone was growing more desperate.

Alongside the roads, the piles of trash were growing, and stories of looting and killing for supplies were everywhere. Many stories were rumors and untrue, but there was some truth to parts of it. Too much truth.

Word had gotten out that the National Guard had been ordered to shoot looters on sight, and there was now a curfew. No travel after dark, for any reason.

This I heard from Jon, who had gone along for the ride into Lancaster.

He had heard more, that masses of people were leaving the cities on foot, that fuel was growing increasingly scarce.

Jon had many stories, and dark news was all about. It feels

as it did when that storm was gathering, like the clouds are fat and bulging and dark.

AT DINNER, MORE BEEF, and there were potatoes that had been brought by from the Sorensons, to whom we had given some cuts of steak. And greens, there were, and fresh milk from the morning. Though it had been cold outside the whole day long, all the bodies gathered and the warmth from the woodstove made the house feel welcoming.

Everyone was gathered around, and the table was cheery, and there was talk about our plans to go to the Stolfutzes' for dinner the next day. There were important things to discuss, especially what sort of pies we should bring to their house tomorrow.

"So should it be apple, or should we make pumpkin pie?" asked Hannah. "I have the sugar and the cinnamon, and we've prepared the dough for the crusts, and we have plenty of both. Who says pumpkin?"

"Pumpkin," Jacob said, "I want pumpkin!" Mike and Derek agreed.

Sadie piped up. "Remember that Mr. Stolfutz has a special favorite! He is always saying that he likes . . ." and her voice hitched. "*Aaaa. Aaaa.*"

And suddenly her body went taut and straight, like a plank laid across her chair. Like the legs of the steer, I thought. Just like the legs of the steer.

Another seizure, so like the throes of death. Her eyes rolled back, and she was choking, choking on the food that was still half chewed in her mouth. Before any of us could move toward her, she toppled off the chair and onto the floor, shaking like a drying sheet in the wind.

Dishes crashed all around, and there was uproar.

I rose quickly, and Hannah let out a cry, but Shauna was with her in a moment. She turned her, and cleared her air pipe, and then held her loosely, protecting her head from the hard tile floor.

Shauna asked if we had any medications we'd been giving her, and we did not. Her antiseizure medication had run out last week, and there was no doctor that could be called, not now.

As she bucked and convulsed, Shauna loosened the top buttons of Sadie's blouse. "She has to breathe. She'll be fine. It'll be all right. She has to breathe."

Her breathing was a gurgling, like thick soup on the stove. But she was breathing.

It could not have lasted more than a minute, but it seemed like it was forever. I knelt by her side, and Hannah by her other, and she began to calm, her body slowly stilling.

Her eyes came into focus, and she looked at me, finally seeing.

"I'm just like him, Dadi. He's just like me." Her voice was weak and faint.

That was all she said, and then she closed her eyes, her breathing easing.

Hannah and Shauna helped take her upstairs and to bed. Hannah stayed with her for a while, and Shauna came back downstairs. We talked for a while, about Sadie's seizures, about the different medicines the doctors had given us.

Shauna seemed to know much about those things, and what she had to say was very reassuring. I found myself thankful that she was here with us.

I WENT TO SIT with Sadie for a little while, as it came time to sleep. She seemed very tired, but not unhappy. As she lay there in her nightdress, we did not speak, but simply sat with one another.

I held her shoulder, gently, and she looked off into the distance, playing with her hair. She teased it, and twisted it, and pulled at it softly.

She began to hum, a tune that I would wordlessly sing to her when she was a little girl. It was a lullaby, one I remember from a video I saw on *rumspringa*. I could not remember the name of the movie, or the name of the song, or even any of the words. But it was simple and beautiful, and so I would sing it to her before sleep. Never with words.

"I remember that tune, Dadi. I keep thinking about it. Did you never remember what it was called?"

I said that I never had.

"That's okay," she said. And she went back to humming it.

I listened, and we sat.

After a few minutes, she stopped.

"Dadi," she said, her voice soft. Her eyes did not seek mine.

"Yes," I said.

"Do you think I'm still sick? You know, that I'm crazy. That I still need the medicine and the doctors and everything?"

I told her I did not know, that I was not sure. And that I hoped she was better.

She looked up at me. "Do you think I'm—something else?"

I sighed, and asked her if she remembered what she had said after the seizure.

"No," she said, and then paused. "No. I don't. But I think it was something bad." She looked down again, and again began to hum.

I asked her why she thought it was something bad.

There was a pause in her humming.

"I don't know. But I felt suddenly frightened, and ashamed, like my heart was breaking. Like I'd done something horrible. I hadn't. It wasn't me, Dadi. It was someone else."

I told her I did not know what she meant, and she nodded back.

"I don't know what I mean either." And she gave a little laugh.

After a while, her voice grew still, and her eyes closed, and the soft breath of sleep folded her up.

I sat with her for a very long while.

HANNAH IS NOT IN our bed now, but sleeps in the room with Sadie. It is partly because Shauna had suggested it, that it would be good to have someone there and listening to

Sadie as she sleeps. Just to check, to be sure that she does not have another seizure.

But I know Hannah is also afraid that this could mean a return to how Sadie was for so long. The crying out. The pain. We had been blessed with this time, this respite, when she was not so broken of soul. I do not wish her to know that time again.

This is not my decision, I know, whether she suffers or not. That is in God's hands. And I am thankful, thankful that she has been well these last weeks.

My prayers, this evening, are that in the grace of God's Providence, he might spare her all of that pain. But what will come will come. It is God's will, and our only task is to bear it with the grace His Son gives us.

I feel so tired.

October 22

Hard to write today. It is hard.

The news came with the sunrise, with Jon. I was checking on the meat in the drying houses, and saw him riding as if the devil himself was chasing him. He had ridden up fast, too fast, dangerously fast, at a wild gallop. He pulled Chestnut up abruptly, and the horse had clearly been driven hard.

He never came this early, never. Tears were streaming down his cold-burned cheeks, but it was not the cold that drew his tears.

He was crying as he told me, sitting there on his horse.

"Isaak Stolfutz is dead," he said, choking out the words.

I felt my legs weaken, as if the tendons had been cut. Isaak? How? I started to speak, but he stammered out more.

"It is not just Isaak. And Jim. And Barbara. And . . ." His throat closed, and he could speak no more.

"O Lord Jesus, what has happened, Jon?" I said. "Tell me what has happened." I found my legs, and helped him down from his horse. He sat, roughly, and struggled to compose himself.

"I was just, I just, I just came from, to . . ." And he had to catch his breath again. I sat with him, and he tried again. It came out in fits and starts.

Last night there had been shooting, just after dusk. Six or seven shots, all together, then several more a few seconds later. We had not heard it, and it was not far away. Strange, I thought, as he told me, that we did not hear it. They are not far off. Isaak's property abuts ours to the north. Just a half mile, no more.

It was the time of Sadie's seizure. It must have been.

Old Jon had told him to ride over to the house, to talk to Isaak, to see if they had heard anything. The shots, they thought, might have come from someone hunting on the Stolfutz property.

But when Jon had cantered up the drive, he found bodies. Right outside of the barn, Isaak and Barbara and little Sophie and Benjamin. Sophie turned seven just four weeks ago. And Benjamin was only ten.

The house was ransacked. Food gone, mostly, but everything smashed up. And in the kitchen, the bodies of the two oldest boys, Jim and Eli. Jim was seventeen, and he and Jon were inseparable. He had been shot in the head. Twice.

I asked about the two middle girls, Maisie and Grace. He just did not know. He was too scared to shout for them, he said, and he had fled.

Jon had ridden straight back home, in a panic, and told his father.

"Dadi told me to tell everyone, to tell everyone to come. He rode to tell Bill Smith, who could get word to the sheriff. And then he will go there himself. He said to get you, you would know what to do."

At that moment, I did not feel that I knew what to do any more than if he had landed a helicopter in the drive and asked me to fly it. But God gives strength and guidance, especially in those times when we feel lost and uncertain.

I told Jon to ride on, to everyone, to do what his father had told him, and gather up as many of the menfolk as he could and to tell them what he had told me. Tell them to come.

"I will ride there with my friend Mike," I said. "We will look around, and see what we can find. Go, now, go."

And he managed to get back on Chestnut, and rode off, nearly as quickly as he had come.

Mike had just walked up, with Derek at his side and Tad loping along behind.

"What's going on?" he asked. I told him there had been a shooting, a neighbor, Isaak. And that there were others dead.

"Isaak? And . . . Barbara? And . . ." He cursed, and shook his head in disbelief. "I'll go get my gun." I knew that he had brought his carbine with him.

I told him that I did not want him to do that. "If you come with me, please do not do that," I said. "I do not wish for there to be any more killing."

He muttered something under his breath, but said he would come with me without it. Derek, too, but Tad said he did not want to. Go get my wife, I told him. Tell her this, and get some of our old sheets. So he did.

I moved, quickly, to go hitch up Nettie to the buggy. Mike helped.

Hannah came out to see me as I was finishing, her face ashen. Behind her, Shauna and Sadie.

"Can it be," she said. "Is this really so?" Barbara was a close friend to Hannah, almost like a sister. "And the children?" Her lips tightened, and her eyes brimmed. "Go. You must go and see."

We spoke a brief prayer together, for strength, for guidance.

And then Mike and Derek and I left in the buggy. I drove Nettie as quickly as I could.

THE THREE OF US arrived, and it was as Jon had said. The farm was very quiet. There the bodies were out in the drive, two large, two so very small. They had fallen together, close to one another, just a heap, like a pile of meat dumped on the road.

Isaak had been my friend, almost from the moment we arrived in this community. He and Barbara had given us welcome, and he had shared his gentle spirit with us. We ate together, we prayed together, we worked side by side. A good and gentle man. And there he was, that strong farmer's body, broken, that fine spirit now gone to be with Christ.

His flesh was cold, and his body was hardening. It had been

many hours. I asked for help with the bodies. Mike helped me separate them, and to cover them, and to close their eyes, but Derek could not help us. He stood back, clenched fist to his mouth, knuckles white.

"Who does this?" whispered Mike, over and over again, as we wrapped the bodies of the children. As if it was the only thought his mind could form. "Who does this?"

When we were finished with the bodies, we did the same with the boys in the house. And then we moved through the farm. I called out the names of the girls, shouting, shouting their names, Maisie! Grace!, over and over. We stayed together, although dividing up would have been best for searching. I think that none of us wanted to be away from the others.

The house was empty, and so much of it had been smashed and broken. Their basement larder, so well stocked, had been completely ransacked. But much else had been simply broken or shattered, just out of anger. Why smash plates? Why break windows?

But for a heart so far fallen from the love of God, breaking things is easy. If you see no value in a soul, why would you see value in a practical thing?

We shouted, and we searched, and when we found them, they were in the barn.

They appeared like wraiths, covered in hay, their dresses dirty and crumpled. Grace was wide-eyed and distant, her older sister walking with her, guiding her. "Here we are," said Maisie. "Here we are."

As I moved toward them, I heard the sound of horses. Others were arriving.

I HAVE FINISHED MY evening's work late and by lamp-light, the task that I did not know I would be given this morning. Mike helped me, his hands working alongside mine.

Six coffins, four large, two small. All pine, from my supply. So simple to build, these boxes. We loaded them onto the wagon, and now I write.

Tomorrow, we will bury them, bury our brothers and sisters in the Stolfutz family plot. It is not on Isaak's farm, but on the farm of his grandfather, which is now part of the Schrock Farm. Bishop Schrock and the deacons decided this.

We cannot wait, as we would, for a decent viewing. That is tradition, and the way of the Order, but we cannot wait. The funeral home has closed, the director gone. He had family in the South, and no one has heard from him in over a week.

Embalming is not possible, and none among the Order know the art well enough. We must move quickly, before the bodies decay. It is cold, so that will help. But it still cannot wait.

Many men arrived after Maisie and Grace made themselves known. There was not much that could be done, and we were careful not to clean until the police came. So there was much prayer, much prayer in that time.

Grace did not speak, it was as if she could not. She was in shock. But Maisie did not want to stop speaking. She told us of what they had seen. They were gathering eggs for dinner from the coop, when a beat-up blue pickup truck pulled in, with six or seven men. They all had guns, and they shouted for food and supplies, waving their guns angrily and saying terrible things.

The girls hid, and watched.

Isaak showed them where the food was, and gave them all that they had. Not just a little, but everything. They took everything from the larder. Then they went into the house.

Some of the men grew angrier and angrier, though Isaak tried to calm them, and told them there was no threat, and that they could have anything they wanted. One man seemed calmer, seemed like he was their leader, and he talked quietly with their father. They made them stand in a circle, then get down on their knees, with their backs to them. Maisie said they went to hide then, as quietly as they could, in the barn, under the hay.

Then came the sound of shooting. Then there was more shooting from inside the house. The men searched and smashed things, but the girls stayed hidden and quiet, deep within the warmth of the hay.

The sheriff came, after an hour, in a four-wheel drive that had been gotten running. Three deputies came with him.

I left shortly after he arrived, my charge in hand. And so after a quiet dinner with prayer, I have built the coffins. Hard, hard thing, it is, to live in these times.

October 23

The cold continues, close to freezing.

I left early, immediately after breakfast, with Mike along in the wagon laden with coffins. Pearl pulled us, strong in her stolid way.

We reached the farm, where a dozen men had stayed overnight to watch over the house and do what they could to prepare and protect the bodies. They were in a row, neatly wrapped in thick cloth. There could be no viewing, not because of decay, even with no embalming. Cold as it had been, that is not a worry. The bullets had done too much damage, and with no one to repair the heads and faces, it would not be good. Better to remember what they had been.

We carefully placed each of them into the caskets, and then together loaded them onto the funeral wagon, which had been brought by the Sorensons.

Then we moved off, one after another, a line of buggies and wagons, a blacksnake creaking along through the fields.

There was little talking as we moved along. Really none at

all. Just the creak of the wheels, and the smell of the horses, and the sound of Pearl's breathing as she pulled the wagon.

There were many other buggies when we reached the Stolfutz plot, a small square of farmland set apart by a white picket fence. Hannah was already there with the children, dressed in black. There were others there, too, a couple of trucks. Outside the fence, benches had been brought, everything the church wagon could carry, plus more from the farms in the community.

It was not enough for all who were there. Many stood, out around the edges.

The graves were already dug, six in a row. Markers had been made, as was our custom, by Jon Thorson's hand, simple stone with the initials of each cut into them.

We laid each of the caskets by one another, a line of them, up on some tables that had been brought. I found my place, alongside Hannah and next to Sadie. I saw that Maisie was sitting with Mrs. Schrock, because the Schrocks had taken the girls in for now. Grace was not there, which was probably for the best. The service began.

It was the same, the same as it always is. The silent prayer. The simple, slow songs. Asa Schrock preached the first message, and then again he preached the second. They were the same as he had preached when Jonas died, the same as he preached whenever anyone died.

Why would they be different? Death comes to us all, as it comes to animals and plants and all things living. It is the same. Asa spoke about God's Providence, about our duty, about serving and being humble and patient no matter the circumstance, about not being prideful. He spoke about how important it was for us to trust, and to stay true.

And about not letting fear take us and change us, turning us away from the simple path of grace. He does not usually say that. But it was a good thing to say. Sadie nestled against my side, but she seemed still and calm, which was good. Hannah held my hand, held it tightly.

Then we sang, and prayed in silence. When the service was done, all filed past the coffins. I had marked the names on each, so that we could know in our leave-taking which we were seeing. There were many people there, and many leaves to be taken, and the line moved slowly.

Afterward, there were sandwiches and tea, very simple. There had not been much time to prepare, but those who had prepared had done their best.

Unlike the Beiler funeral, there was not much talking. Jonas had his leave-taking, even though that cancer moved so terrible quick. But so many all at once was very hard, particularly on the children.

Even though we know it is God's will, and that God will care justly for one who lives a righteous life, it is not easy to have so many friends no longer with us.

It goes deeper than that, I think.

Because we know, now, that as the world of the English fails around us, we are not separate. Yes, we have the Order, and yes, we have our way, but the time when that meant we stood free from the world has passed.

I am not sure, as I think about it now, if that has ever been true. We are never really apart, as much as we choose to set ourselves different from the world that surrounds us.

The English are like the earth, or the air. And if the rain falls, it falls on all alike, as the Bible says.

As WE WERE EATING the simple meal afterward, in that somber visiting, I found myself talking with Bill Smith, who had come to pay his respects. He was shaken, because Isaak was a neighbor and a good friend. He'd heard the shots, and he'd gone out to check his herd, because people were starting to steal cattle.

"I shoulda known," he said. "I shoulda checked on him, shoulda known something bad had happened. You just can't imagine that it'd be something like this, bad as it is."

I agreed but told him there was no way he could have known. And if he had known, what could he have done?

He nodded. "Yeah. I suppose you're right."

I asked after his family, how they were coping.

"Donna'd wanted to come," he said, his voice husky and strained. "But she was just too much a mess this morning. It's hard enough with Isaak and Barbara. The kids, though. Man, they were such good kids. I just don't know how we came to this."

I said that I knew God's hand would carry us through this time, but that it would not be easy.

"No, no it won't. But you have to know folks around here aren't going to take this lying down. You folk are a blessing to us all, and I know we've got different ways, but we just can't sit by and watch evil men hurt you and your kids. You know we just can't."

I told him that I would pray for him, but it was hard to hear those words from him. More anger, more violence, building and building. More armed men, even friends, could not be a good thing.

The sword has no handle, as Jonas Beiler used to say. When you take it up, the blade cuts into your hand. But now the sword is all around us. It seems to be everywhere, like a sharp harvest rising from the fields. It will touch us, whether we choose it or not.

October 24

Still cold this morning, close to a frost, so much colder than it was this time last year.

I look at my journal, and on this day last year it was almost eighty degrees. And the year before, eighty-two. But the year before was cold. So difficult to predict. I don't know if those three acres of wheat will make it, not if it gets much colder. Already, the storm damage and the cold have taken a toll. That will be a loss, if it is so. The flour is most needed.

Dr. Jones came by a little before noon, riding on his bicycle. The message had gotten to him about Sadie, and he came by to look at her.

We talked for a while, and he offered his condolences, and said that Sadie seemed fine. She was in good spirits, though she seemed always to be humming that tune. We gave him some dried beef, and prayed with him a little, and he left us with some medication.

"I don't have much left," he said. "And I don't know when I'll be getting any more. So use it if she gets worse."

Young Jon did not come today. I realized it as the afternoon wore on, and there was no news. It was hard for him, I think. Seeing that death. It was hard for me. I hope that he will come again, and come soon.

As dusk came, a party of men could be seen in the darkness, walking the road, alongside a cart that was drawn by a horse. They were not simple folk, but as they grew closer, I realized that I knew many of them. They were neighbors, all of them, a dozen or more.

All were armed, mostly with rifles. They waved as they passed.

In the night, there are sounds from Sadie's room. A thumping and a rustling, and I wake, to go and see what it is that she is doing. She is stirring in her sleep, and I am so alert, so aware of it that I cannot help but wake. I move down the hall, and open her door just a crack.

In the bed, in the half-light, I can see her shifting and twisting slowly in her covers. But she is not crying out, not struggling to breathe or screaming in the darkness. It is just a small voice, spoken from sleep. There are not words, though they sound like words.

And in there, for a moment, and then again, there is that tune.

I must remember where I heard it.

October 25

Sabbath today, and I feel spent. It is the funeral, I think, that
has left my soul feeling depleted and empty. I felt the absence
of Isaak, before we left, as we arrived at the Sorensons', and
throughout the service.

There was nothing different, nothing wrong, nothing
flawed with the service. There never is. Simple, and as con-
stant as a stone. It was as it is. But some days, my spirit is weak
in me. I feel absent and without strength.

Yet still I go, and still I am part of it, and still I do not question that I am there. That is the strength of being part of the
Order, of letting it be your guide. You go when you are joy-
ful. You go when you are not. And by this, you find yourself
standing on a firm foundation.

AT THE END OF the service, the deacons spoke to all
gathered, about Isaak. It was Deacon Sorenson, mostly, as the
others watched and listened. He told us about how word had
been sent to Isaak's younger brother, in Ohio. We would try

to find a way to get Maisie and Grace to their family, and if it was God's will, it would be so.

Then Bishop Schrock reminded us all that Isaak was one commissioned to preach, and that in losing him, we had lost a preacher. That would need to change, and the deacons had met to select another.

It can be done by choice, or it can be done by simple lot, but Asa said the choice was clear.

And he spoke my name.

I nodded, and acknowledged it.

It was not what I wanted to hear today, but perhaps it is always that way. Among the English, being a preacher meant you were important, that you were a leader. Here, it is a task. It is a simple demand of the Order. It is like plowing a field, or butchering a cow.

I hope that, for me, it is not too much like butchering a cow.

AFTER DINNER, WHICH SHAUNA and Mike had prepared for us while we went to worship, Mike wanted to talk with me. We stepped out into the night, and walked the drive.

"Are things still holding together, Jacob?"

I told him that I wasn't sure what he meant.

"I mean, are you going to have enough. I know you say it. Shoot, I think you believe it. But Shauna and I been talking tonight, you know, about us staying here. It's been so good, and you and Hannah have been so good for us."

I told him it had been good for us, too.

"But really, Jacob, we've been down in the larder, looking at what you have here. How can it possibly work? We're so many to feed. Maybe we should think about finding somewhere—"

I stopped him. My words back to him were plain. Where? Where would they go? There was nowhere, nowhere in the world that was not like this. If they left, they would face hardship. Here, they were family. They were our strength. Things were easier with them here. "You fill this house, Mike," I said. "You fill it."

And he knew what I meant.

Had he been the sort of man to embrace, he would have embraced me there.

I HAVE WOKEN AGAIN to gunfire. It is early morning, maybe two or three o'clock, and the night pops and crackles with it. It is distant, but it goes on for ten minutes, and it is the most that I can remember hearing. Hannah woke up with it, too, and together we spent those ten minutes in prayer. For our family, for God's grace, for whoever was out there in the night facing death. After it stopped, she went back to bed, but I find that I am still awake.

Now I write, but I must sleep. I simply must.

I HAD FALLEN BACK asleep, I don't know when, maybe four o'clock, and there was banging at the door of the house. I woke with a start, and made my way downstairs through the cold house. Now? At this time of night? My heart raced, as it will when you are woken suddenly. Hannah woke, too, and I tried to tell her that she should stay upstairs.

She would have none of that, and came down with me to see who was at the door. I told her that she should not come, should be prepared to hide and take the children, but she scoffed at me.

"It could not be men with ill intent, Jay. Don't be foolish," she said. "We do not have locks on our doors. Why would they knock, when they could come right in."

She was right. That's the most difficult thing about marrying a smart woman.

We came downstairs, each bearing a lantern, and went to the door.

I swung the door wide, and in the faint light of the lamp, there was a circle of men's faces out on the porch. My eyes struggled with the darkness, but I could immediately see that all of them were armed, and again my heart bolted like a horse in my chest.

I realized one was Bill Smith. It was a relief to see his face, I will admit. The other looked a little familiar, but I could not remember his name. Thomas, maybe. He was from Lititz, and I rarely had any dealings with him.

Standing in the drive, there were four more, shotguns and rifles in hand, leashed dogs snuffling around their feet.

I asked Bill what was happening.

"We caught up with the men who killed Isaak and his family, Jacob," he said. "Down at the Johanson farm. Nobody'd been checking in there for a few days, and I guess the place looks abandoned enough that they figured they could just settle in. When we were doing the sweep, one of the guys noticed that there was a truck there didn't belong, looked like that old blue truck the Stolfutz girl told the sheriff about."

"Was that the shooting?" I asked.

"Yeah. We got ahold of the sheriff and a couple of deputies, he deputized the lot of us, and we went down there. There was about six of 'em, looks like they'd been there for a day or more. We waited and watched, and called in more folks until the place was locked down right good.

"They went out to the truck at about two-thirty, middle of the night, all of them, all armed. I figure they were heading out to hit another house. No way that was happening. We couldn't let 'em do that, so we, well, yeah. When they pulled out down the road, we were waiting. A couple of our guys were hurt, but we got pretty much all of 'em."

"Dead?" I asked.

"Well, mostly. That's why we're here. A couple of them made it into the fields, jumped from the truck and took off on foot. The fields were pretty overgrown, and they managed to lose us. Thought we might have winged one, but I don't think we can be sure. We got guys out there with dogs now, and we're going to be checking in your fields, wanted to let you know what's up. They're around and they're armed, and they've killed before."

I nodded. I told them they were welcome to search.

"'Preciate it. And we're also just letting y'all know to keep a watch out. If you see anything, just get word to my house, and folks will get word to us. We just want to be sure that no one else around here gets hurt, no more kids, no more Old Order people, nobody."

I told him we would keep our eyes open.

"Seriously, Jacob. Be careful. Stay away from danger."

A half smile came to my face. "We do. But we can't seem to keep it from coming to us."

He shook his head. I thanked him for his efforts to watch out for us.

"Thanks, Jacob."

He took a half step down, but that moment, the dogs began barking, barking fiercely and pulling at their leads. The guns came up, but it was just Mike, coming out of the *daadi haus* to see what was happening.

He offered to lend a hand, said he had a rifle and knew how to use it, and asked if he could come along. Bill nodded, and said they could always use an extra hand and set of eyes. Mike ran back to the *daadi haus*, and returned with that carbine of his.

And they were off again, Mike with them, walking back down into the darkness. Hannah and I returned to bed.

IT'S BEEN A COUPLE of hours, and Hannah is back asleep. I am not, though. The dogs were barking for a while, and I was aware of Bill and the other deputies as they moved through the fields, but they moved on over an hour ago. I am simply awake, and I do not feel like reading. I feel I need to write about all this, to chronicle this uncertain time.

Outside the window, the first of the morning light is beginning to stain the sky. I will be tired today. Hard to be focused, when you have not slept. But focused or not, the cattle must be fed, the pigs must be fed, and work must be done.

October 26

Today blended with yesterday, like the sunrise slowly becoming day. I was weary all day, and I could feel myself moving more slowly as I worked.

It is like working while sick, when much has to be done and a cold has taken you. You simply get done what you need to, but at a different pace. Hannah was patient with me, and having Mike's family with us made the morning go more smoothly. Mike came back in the early morning, rested, and then left again to join the deputies in their searching. We gave him food to sustain himself. He said he would be gone until they'd found the men, and there was a grimness in his voice.

Jon came by again, cantering up on Chestnut. It was good to see him riding again, and sharing what he had learned, although there was not much that was really new, of course. We had already heard everything last night. But it was good to see him.

It is late afternoon now, and I am too tired to write more. I will rest, for a short while.

THEY CAME AT DUSK.

I was at the front of the house grooming Nettie when they moved out of the shadows, the two of them, both lean and intent. One was taller, rangy, his eyes sleepy and lidded. The other moved behind him like a ghost, a full head shorter. The tall one carried a long gun, exactly like the ones the soldiers carry. The smaller one held an automatic pistol in one hand. He held Jacob in the other. His hand was tightly wrapped around Jacob's upper arm, and I could see that Jacob was struggling not to cry out.

The tall one looked at me, with eyes that both saw me and didn't see me.

"We need food," he said, in a smooth, easy voice. "Hard times, eh? Folks gotta do what they gotta do, and right now, you gotta help us." He smiled, and gestured toward Jacob with the rifle. His eyes were not smiling at all. "Right?"

I told him that we had food in our larder, and that he was welcome to take what he needed. As I said this, I heard an exhalation from behind me, and it was Hannah, standing on the steps to the kitchen.

"Why don't you come down over here, ma'am," the sleepy-eyed man said, smoothly and politely. "Who else you got here?" he asked. "You folks do have big families, don'tcha?"

I did not say anything, but it was then that Sadie appeared with a basket of eggs. She did not seem startled or upset, and when the man waved for her to come over and join us, she did so quietly.

"Any other family kicking around?" he asked. "I don't like surprises, you know."

I told him that this was all of our family. I did not lie. I hoped, in that moment, that Shauna and Derek and Tad would stay quiet and out of sight.

The tall man hurled a duffel bag toward us. "You and the boy go get us as much food as you can put in this bag. We'll stay here to keep an eye on the ladies. Don't you take long, now. I'm kinda in a hurry." He grinned again.

I told him that we would go quickly and get what they needed, and he nodded. "Y'all are such helpful people."

Jacob and I ran to get the food, and quickly filled the bag with supplies from the larder. We did not speak, and Jacob looked ashen.

We returned with the bag, and when we did, he motioned for Hannah and Sadie to come stand by us.

"Have the boy bring it over here," said the tall one, as the smaller one kept his pistol trained on us. Jacob did, and then was sent back over to stand with us. The tall man took a look at the bag, carefully examining the contents. Canned vegetables and soups, and enough jerky for two men for days. "Jerky, huh?" Again, the smile. "Thanks, man. I love me some jerky."

"Let's get out of here, Jim," said the smaller one, in an anxious voice that crackled and broke.

The rangy man gave him a slow, pointed look. "You giving the orders now?"

"No, no, man, but I . . ." And he fell silent.

"Yeah. That's what I thought." He passed the duffel bag to the smaller man, who shouldered it.

"But he does have a point, doesn't he? It's time for us to

get going." He looked at me, as serene as a serpent. "Course, folks are looking for us, and it just won't do for you to tell 'em which way we went. So I'm gonna ask you to turn around, get on your knees, and then close your eyes and count to a thousand. Nice and easy. You can do that for me, right?"

Sadie slipped her hand into mine at that moment, and looked at me. "Dadi," she said. "You know his heart, Dadi."

And with her eyes meeting mine, I knew what this man intended. I felt it with certainty. In the emptiness of his eyes, I could see him saying just that very thing to Isaak. I could see it just as surely as if I had been standing there when he had them kneel, and then killed them.

I took Hannah's hand with my other, and held it tightly. Jacob stood by her side.

I could feel my heart racing in my chest, but I managed not to let the trembling enter my voice.

"Leaving is not the only thing you mean to do now, is it?" I said this, and I looked at him. "We will not raise a hand to stop you, but neither will we look away."

He uttered a short, resigned curse, and then raised the rifle, as the other lowered his head and stared at the ground. Hannah's hand closed hard on my own, and I heard her whispering the Lord's Prayer.

"Whatever," he said, shaking his head, the smile fixed in place.

And there was a roar like a blow, and another, and another, four in all, fast and close. Hannah let out a short, breathless gasp.

The tall man's smile was gone. As was much of the tall man's head, and he fell like a toppled tree. He lay on the ground, legs out straight and twitching. The other fell, too, with a crashing of jars. He writhed and cried out, a gurgling, strangled cry.

There, by the workshop, stood Derek, pale as a sheet. In his hands he held my father's pistol. He took a half step back, and then vomited.

Shauna was suddenly there. "Oh my God oh my God oh my God," she said, over and over again.

Sadie moved away from me, like a ghost, past the body of the dead man and to the one who lay struggling for life on the ground.

The smaller man was dressed in fatigues and a dark, heavy jacket, which were draped over his thin frame. Whippet thin he was, probably in the best of times. His breathing was a wet struggle, jagged inhalations, rough breaths, his eyes wild and unseeing.

Derek had hit him in the chest. His head was resting on Sadie's lap, and her light blue dress was stained with his blood.

"He's hurt so bad, Dadi," she said, matter-of-factly. "I do not think that he will live."

I looked at him, and though I am not a doctor, I had to agree with her.

"I wonder if he has a name. He seems very young," Sadie said.

She was right. His hair was long and dirty, hanging matted over his face. As she swept it away, I saw that he was only a few years older than she, the edge of his sunken face barely traced with stubble, a wisp here and there of light beard. He was barely a man, barely older than Derek.

Shauna ran to the *daadi haus*, then returned with her kit. She settled in next to Sadie, and pulled up his shirt slightly to examine the wound. He did not flinch, or even shift, but just continued with his ragged, shallow breathing. Under the shirt, it was a terrible mess, and Shauna covered it up again.

She looked up at me. "Can't do anything for this," she said. Her face was pale.

I nodded, and Sadie asked if we should move him, and maybe try to get the doctor. "It can't help," said Shauna. "But we can try to make him more comfortable. Not long, I think."

"Should I go try to find my dad and the sheriff?" asked Derek, his voice shaky. I said he could if he wanted to, and he nodded. Tell him one is dead, and that the boy will not live, I instructed him.

So Derek left, and we stayed with the boy, as the darkness spread across the sky and the air grew cold.

Hannah brought blankets from the house, and food for us. We covered him as we could, but he was past the need for food and drink. We prayed both out loud and in silence. There was nothing else that could be done, but pray and be there with him.

Sadie would not leave him, not for a moment. And he lingered. His body was broken, but it must have been young and strong before hunger wasted it and the bullet tore at it. An hour passed, and still he breathed. The night grew deeper, and the chill pressed in. She spoke to him, softly, about the trees and the stars and the sky. About forgiveness.

After a while, his body tensed, his breath became a rasp, deepening, clutching at the cold of the night.

And then Sadie's voice was that little singsong tune, wordless, meaningless, comforting. She sang, and she sang, and then she stopped. And he grew stiller, and the breath hissed away like steam into the night, and he was dead.

"He and me, Dadi." She set his head down gently, and put her face close to his ear. "*Vi miah dee fagevva vo uns shuldich sinn,*" she said, in a soft voice that carried. *As we forgive those who sin against us.* Then she stood, and walked to the house.

I sent Tad for the handcart, and for some sheets for the corpses. We are keeping them in the barn tonight.

It has taken a long time for my hands to grow warm enough to write this. They still feel so cold, and they will not stop shaking. But I do not think they shake only because of the cold.

October 27

We buried the man and the boy in the morning, after the sheriff and a deputy came to see the bodies and talk with us.

It was a bitter day, bright with sun, cold and sharp. A light frost lay on the grass, and the wind came in ragged gusts.

We had wrapped the bodies in sheets for burial. Their blood had stained the sheets a deep umber, here and there. We used the handcart to move them back to a stand of trees on the southern edge of the pasture, and there Mike and I and Derek began to dig. The others stayed in the house.

The ground was near frozen, hard and unyielding, and the work was slow going. We labored in silence, only the sounds of our shovels against the soil.

I looked up from my work, and there was Sadie. I had not heard her come, or seen her.

She was kneeling by the shrouded corpse of the boy, her back to me. In her slight voice, she was singing that lullaby again, with words that meant nothing to me.

She was not wearing her *kapp* on her head, and the wind

played with her long hair, twisting it, tangling it. I set down my shovel, and walked to her, and put my hand on her shoulder.

The wind rose up, stinging my face.

The air filled with leaves, torn down from the trees by the thousands. Like rain, dancing down all around us, brown and brittle. They filled the air, hissing, like dried cat bones through the sky. They eddied over the opened ground of the grave, and skittered like the husks of insects across the shroud.

One caught in Sadie's hair. She reached back, absently, thoughtlessly, took it, and then closed her pale, delicate fingers around it.

It crumbled like nothing in her hand. Then she opened her hand, and the pieces leapt away in the wind.

Her head turned to me, and her eyes were bright.

"Oh, Dadi," she said.

October 28

This morning, I felt so tired. Like the life was out of me, like my heart was full of molasses. I woke, but it was hard.

Mike was up, and a good help, and Shauna was in the kitchen with Hannah. Tad is helping Jacob. Derek was with Sadie, helping with the milking and her other chores.

I did what needed to get done, but my thoughts kept returning to that boy. And that man. I will not ever know their names, I don't think. The man, like a wolf, his eyes just filled with simple violence.

But the boy? It was like Sadie said. He was just a boy. And yet there he was, living because of the hate of the man, being fed by the violence. I cannot stop thinking about it, and it is distracting me. I read and reread what I wrote yesterday, about burying him. I see the bloody sheet, feel the hardness of his body.

I must stop writing now. I must stop reading now. There is work I must do.

SADIE HAD VISITORS THIS afternoon, Liza Schrock and Rachel Fisher, as have so often come. But others, too, a dozen. Almost every wife of the community, and some of the girls. And Shauna. She was there, and my Hannah. They sat in the grass out by where the late-season kale still grows, women all in a circle.

Sadie seemed calm, at ease, different than she had been. It was hard to say in what way, but she did.

I could not hear most of what they were saying, but there was much talking. What I heard, a snippet here as I passed, was about the boy and his dying. They huddled and leaned in close as Sadie talked, like being gathered around a campfire on a cold night. I saw that Shauna was crying, but I could not tell why. Others were crying, too. Hannah looked distant, sad in the way she shows her sorrow, by going deep inside.

I felt like a busybody watching them, and there was a pig to be slaughtered, so I went about my business.

I TALKED TO SADIE, there in the kitchen, as she was preparing dinner. Hannah was distracted, slow, moving the way that I have felt these last two days. Sadie, though, seemed fine. Just peeling potatoes, quick and nimble, just like everything was normal.

I asked her what it was about, what the women wanted to hear from her.

She looked at me, and her eyes were sad.

"Oh, Dadi, you know. You know what some people think. That I know things."

I asked her if she did.

She sighed, and her hands paused in their task. "It's like sometimes my soul is all lit up, like lightning on a summer night, in a cloud without rain." She suddenly looked very old.

I told her she hadn't answered my question.

Her eyes flitted downward, to the potato in her hand. "I know I haven't."

I asked again. "What were you telling the women?"

"I think we have to go."

"Go where?" I asked.

"To where it isn't safe."

I was going to ask what that meant, but Hannah came over, and chided me for distracting Sadie.

"Dinner's got to be made, Jay. Let a woman do her work!" She tried to say it with humor, but she just sounded tired and frustrated.

So I let them work.

October 29

Last night, distant gunfire woke me twice. *Tocktocktocktock-tock*, like many men nailing boards in a barn all at once. It went on for a while each time. I had trouble returning to sleep. Fortunately, Hannah slept through it.

It was cool this morning, neither hot nor cold. There was no frost in the ground. So hard to predict. This time last year, it was hot every day. And now I worry about the last of the crops, the greens and the late potatoes, but the frost has not yet taken them.

They have not been easy, these last days. I find myself still so distracted, so full of myself and my own pride. I know that there is work to do, that I have my duty to perform. But I feel weakened. Bloodless. My mind is listless, and this is not good.

Twice now this morning, I found myself here with this diary in my hand. I sit and I read, when I know there is work to be done. I am reading back, and seeing the picture of the boy in my mind's eye. I wonder who he might have been, among the English. I wonder about who his parents were, and when they last saw him.

I think of Hannah's hand, tightening in my own. Her gasp. I see the man fall, and hear the ragged breath of the boy, and smell the scent of his blood in the air. I can see the tremble in my hand as I wrote about it, how my letters are shaky and uncertain. I feel my hands, cold as they wrote it. Reading it, I feel that day again, just as strong.

Maybe stronger. It is like alcohol, as the memory ferments in me.

AFTER THE WORK OF the early day was done, I took Nettie and rode to visit Asa in the late morning. I wanted to talk, hear what Liza was telling him, and ask about what he was thinking.

As I rode, I passed a man walking. He was very thin, like a rail, and his many layers of clothes were dirty. He wore a backpack, heavy with things. It looked like it had been very nice once, and his boots were fancy hiking boots, expensive in the way of the English. Or they had been. Now they were as dirty as his face.

"Can you spare anything," he asked, in a voice that was frail and brittle. "Please. It's been days. I . . . please." He looked furtive. Ashamed.

I had a couple of apples, brought for my lunch, and some meat. I gave him one of the apples, and he was thankful. He ate it carefully, slowly. It seemed that it hurt him to eat, perhaps his teeth. And it was a firm apple.

I asked him his name, and where he was from, and he told me.

Doug. From Philly. He was thirty-two, and his parents lived

in Florida. He used to be a vice-president of a company that used to do things with investing. I don't remember exactly.

His girlfriend was, he said, nearby, where they'd set their tent. Too tired from nights and days of walking. She must be hungry too, I said, so I offered him half of the meat I had brought, and he hesitated.

"She . . . she's a veeg." He paused, like his throat had closed around the word.

"A veeg?" I asked.

"She doesn't . . . eat . . . um . . ." And he seemed to be struggling with something.

"Are you sure you don't want it?" I asked.

He took the jerky, and thanked me.

He asked if there was work, if he could do anything else for food. I told him I did not have need, but that maybe others might. He seemed resigned. I rode on, and when I glanced back for a moment, he was just standing where we had spoken.

THE NEWS, WITH THE cold, grows worse. I heard it from Asa, as we sat out on his porch. The cities, they are emptying. There are too many people, too many hungry and without light for too long, and the efforts to rebuild are too slow. Though there are curfews and many soldiers, and some food coming in from the mostly lost harvest, there is still so much violence. And hunger.

From Philadelphia to the east, from Baltimore in the south, the people are coming.

Asa told me of roads filled with the starving and those who prey on the starving, leaving the cities where there was not enough, leaving and just walking. He told me also of deaths and gunfire, everywhere.

"I was talking to the Guard yesterday. They have set out barricades, Jacob," Asa said. "It's not just the sheriffs and the police. Not just the state Guard. But our neighbors. They want to turn them back, these people, these hungry people. It is like trying to stop the flow of a river, or to catch every falling leaf before it touches the ground."

I thought of Sadie, then, and the leaf crumbling in her hand.

I asked if he had heard the shooting last night, and he said he had, but that he didn't know what exactly had happened.

I told him about the man I passed on the road. Asa nodded.

"There were two families that came to our door yesterday, and we fed them what we could. They made their way past the roadblocks during the night, I think. So hungry. Hollow eyes. Overnight, a half-dozen or so more tents, out on the edge of the wheat field. They came to my door, begged for anything we could give them.

"And in the eastern and northern districts, I hear there are even more tents. They come by the hundreds. There are more, so many more. Maybe thousands. They are still coming, even though they are cold and there is danger, they are coming."

"What can we do?" I asked.

"I don't know, Jacob. I . . ."

He paused, his lips pursing, tight. "I know how to run a

good farm. I know how to serve God, and how to submit to God's will. I try to be a good husband. But I am not sure what we are meant to do. We are *safe* here, I know that." He said it strangely, spitting it out.

Safe? I was surprised. What about Isaak? What about . . .

"We are safe. There is what is left of the police, though more and more go to protect their families, because there is no pay. The sheriff came by, after the shooting at your home. He has almost no one still with him. He has vehicles, but what use are they? Unless you are military, it is too hard to get fuel, too hard to get around, and the police fear for their own families when they are away. So there are the militias now. They will . . . protect us." But he did not say it like a celebration. The words held no reassurance. His lips pursed tighter still, and his eyes dropped from mine. "Is that what we are meant to be, Jacob? Safe? Safe behind the guns of our neighbors?"

Again, he paused. "Jonas would have known what to do. What was it he said? About the sword?"

"It has no handle," I replied.

Asa nodded, still with his eyes down. "I think it cuts us, even if it is not our hand that wields it."

SADIE CAME INTO BED with us tonight. The work of the day was done, and Mike and his family had settled into the *daadi haus* for the evening.

The door opened, as I read and as Hannah knitted. It was like when she was a little girl, her small face around the side of the door.

"What's the matter?" Hannah asked.

"I can't sleep," she said. "I feel . . ." and she stopped talking. Her eyes were bright, and she seemed nervous. But she was not upset in that way she used to be.

Hannah welcomed her over, and she curled up by her side, nestling in like a kitten. I remember, as a boy, wanting that comfort on the nights when the storms rose. My father made it clear that it was not right for a boy to do so, and that waking them would bring the belt.

I am glad our bed is different.

Sadie closed her eyes, and there were more gunshots, closer still than last night. Ten or fifteen, and then silence. Hannah looked at me, quiet. But Sadie did not stir.

Now, they both sleep.

And I sit here, and I watch them. So soft, so quiet.

Safe.

October 31

I did not have time to write yesterday.

It was a warmer day, much warmer, almost hot.

Jon came, riding, with the news of the bodies. His face was grim, and he did not seem to wish to linger. There were five of them, strung from the branches of an old oak near the Sorenson place. They had been shot in the night, then their bodies hung.

"They caught them stealing food," Jon said. Some of the people from the road, trying to steal from a barn. It was full of the feed-corn that had been harvested for the cattle and the pigs with a harvester that's been gotten running. One of the militias caught them, they thought. Then left the bodies out as a warning.

And the tents that had been out on the edge of the Schrocks' wheat field had been smashed. All cut up, things tossed out all around. There was no sign of the families Asa had spoken of.

No one was talking about it. No one knew anything.

Jon told me that a couple of men were going to go cut

down the bodies at noon. It was not good to have them there, where children and others could see them, and where the crows could peck at them. He said that he was going to go, too. He looked less young when he said that, less like the boy who rode so excited to share the news. As he spoke, I could see that his had become a man's face.

He rode off, to tell others. I went in and told Hannah, and said I would go help bury these men. She said it was the right thing to do. I also talked to Mike about the farm work today, asked if he and his boys could tend to what needed tending. He said that he could.

So later that morning, I went.

Jon was there, and his father, and Joseph Fisher. Joseph had brought ladders. I had a shovel. There were several of the English around, too, five or six men I did not recognize. They were carrying long guns. There were no police.

The dead were on two of the middle branches, hung up by ropes, six or seven feet in the air. Four were men. One was not yet a man, though he was tall for his age.

Two had signs, handwritten on cardboard, tied around their necks, just as that first hung body. LOOTER, one of the signs said. THEIF, said another. It was not spelled correctly.

I did not know four of them.

But the one with the sign that said THEIF I knew. It was Doug. From Philly.

His head lolled, his eyes were open, his thin face distended. His feet were bare and blackening, the hiking boots gone.

"We should cut these bodies down," I said.

"Aye," said Joseph Fisher, and he pulled his stepladder from the wagon. I took it, and moved to begin with the man whose name I knew.

There was a shifting among the English men, and one stepped forward. "The bodies oughta stay up. Can't have no thieves takin' what little we got." He shifted the rifle in his arms, but he did not raise it.

I felt my heart race, but I do not think I showed it.

I set the ladder up, and with the help of both Jons I began to take the body of Doug from Philly down. I cut away the rope with my knife, and took the weight as we eased him down. He was rigid, the hardness of death set in, but also light, much lighter than I would have thought for a man of his height. A bag of bones, with no meat. I had not known, under all of those clothes, that he was so thin. How hungry he must have been.

As we worked, Joseph was talking to the men, quietly. They were not happy, but seemed to hear when Joseph said that the bodies would be bad for the children to see.

We buried them, the boy and the three men and Doug from Philly, right there under the oak tree. The ground was softer than it had been before, more eager to take the bodies.

AGAIN, ALL ARE ASLEEP, but I am not. I need sleep, but though I read and I pray, I feel too awake. My mind paces the floor.

There are shots now and again, bursts here and there, far away, and I cannot sleep. I think of this man in his hunger, shot like a rabbit raiding a garden. For what, Lord? For stealing corn intended for pigs and for cattle, like the hungry prodigal helpless in a strange land.

I can hear his voice.

I read back to what I wrote earlier today, and I can hear his voice as I read the words. And I can see the sign, hung around his neck. Not even the right spelling, for this man who has been killed, like a sign above a cross that reads IMRI. I can see him, feel his weight, smell the early rot of him.

Just as I see the man fall, and hear the ragged breath of the boy, and taste the scent of his blood in the air. Those words, and the reflection on those words, like shouting in an empty grain silo. I read back, and back, through the days, and suddenly these pages feel like a terrible burden.

I feel angry at them, and my hand shakes again as I write. I feel an urge to tear out the pages. How silly, to be angry at a book. But I am.

I am angry at the memory it holds, like a band of steel around my chest. A band of words and thoughts, and my soul feels scattered.

And tomorrow is Sunday. I have to preach tomorrow, over at the Schrocks'.

It has begun to rain outside, hard and heavy, clattering against the window.

I try to think about what I might say, as I look at scripture, but my thoughts are as scattered as the rain.

O, Lord.

November 1

It is late again, and I am very tired.

We woke, and brought the food that had been prepared for the meal. Mike and Shauna and the boys woke, too, as they have been doing, and ate a simple meal with us before we left for worship. They promised to tend to some things when we were away.

The ride to the Schrocks' was difficult. All night, it had rained, and a half-mile from their farm, the road had been washed out. Like a bite taken out of the side of an apple, the damage had begun during the big storm, and with every rain, it failed further, and now there was barely room to pass with a buggy. We slowed, and I had everyone get out, and I walked Nettie past it.

Worship was what it was. The old songs, just so. The voices raised, honest and simple. I spoke about the prodigal, about times of hardship in a strange land, about the need to accept what must come, just as the prodigal accepted whatever came to him.

All sat in silence, and their eyes watched me, and now and again there would be a murmur. There sat Hannah and Sadie and Jacob. There sat everyone I know, all listening and still but for the rustling of their movement and the occasional cough.

I talked and I talked, until the words felt like they were done, and then I stopped. It was not like writing, not like thinking about what words might be best. I felt a blur, like I was floating. The Lord will do with the words what He will. I am not sure I even remember what I said. Out the words tumbled, one after another, forgotten the moment their sound had left the air.

I wish all forgetting came as easily.

But then we sang, and we sang some more, the old songs from the *Ausbund*. "Live Peaceably, Said Christ the Lord," we sang, and I felt the roots of that music set my soul more at rest.

After, there was food and there was visiting, but there was something else. Asa asked for the menfolk to gather, and to talk about what must happen next. Word had come to him, he said, from last night. Fifteen dead in Lancaster, at least, in an attack on an army supply convoy. Another dozen on the road from Philly, some refugees, and five men from Lititz who were on the barricade. To the south of Lancaster, a growing city of tents and makeshift shelters, with hundreds and hundreds, many armed. And the word from those around? The militias were meeting, planning. Growing more angry, and more anxious.

There was concern in other districts, especially those more reliant on businesses with English clients, where there were fewer farms and fewer gardens. Most districts had food enough, but many could see that even what they had would not carry through the winter.

And he spoke more, about what he was hearing from the colonel of the National Guard. About the conditions in the cities. What food was available. What fuel was available. How many millions must be fed, and how the numbers were not matching. There would be starvation and famine. It could not be avoided. It would be a terrible, violent winter.

In New Wilmington, the word came that the Plain folk had been overrun, their homes and barns looted. Three wagons bearing two families had arrived at a distant relative's house in a northern district two nights ago, and bore the ill tidings. Many were dead, even though they had offered no resistance.

There were more stories, none of them good.

Asa talked about all of this simply, as if he were sharing details of a new collection for a family in need, or about a barn raising.

"We all knew this would be a time of hardship, and of trouble. We knew it would be hard as winter approached. But to lose a family, and to have blood spilled on our soil? To 'protect us'? And it will happen again, more and more. To know that we cannot feed those who are hungry? What do we think is the Lord's will in this?"

There was silence for a few moments.

Then Joseph spoke up. "You know what Jacob's Sadie has been saying. My wife tells me, what the women are talking about."

Eyes turned to me, with more interest than when I was trying to preach. I had even fewer words. What did I know?

Asa saw that I had no idea what they were talking about, and in mercy spoke up. "Liza has told me, too. About what your Sadie says will be next, when the women have gathered to talk. That we go west, to Ohio, or perhaps beyond, all together with all that we can carry. That we leave this behind. That we leave the safety of Pharaoh and his chariots, and go to where the land is empty and we do not need the blood of others shed so that we might live."

There was murmuring, quietly, among those gathered.

"I have been thinking the same thing. As have others, in other settlements around this district."

There was a faint smile on his face, so rare for Asa. "Not that your young one is telling us what to do. Just seeing what may be."

Joseph looked at me, and asked me what I thought.

I said I was not sure, but that here in this place, the cost was too high. I said I did not know where we could go. I was silent, and thought, for a moment, of my father and my uncle, farther from the great cities. But I could not imagine turning to such a harsh place for solace. Those there would not be welcoming.

It was Asa who spoke up next, about his nephews in Ohio.

And farther yet, of a new settlement in Nebraska. Much land. Good land, abandoned by the English, left to the great machines and robotic harvesters run by the big businesses.

Levi Stolfutz, Isaak's brother, spoke up. He did not often speak, but he was a thoughtful man. "We could reach Ohio in two weeks, which we could make with supplies at hand. And my uncle is there, too, Asa. The community is large. It would be hard, the journey. And they might not be ready. But if we do not leave now, winter will be upon us, and the time to act will have passed."

There was much talking, and back and forth, as others worried about the dangers of the journey, and the even greater peril—to our souls—if we stayed. Then, there was quiet as we thought and prayed.

Asa said that we should pray some more with our families, but that all should gather at his farm again on Tuesday.

And now I am too tired to write more. Even the gunshots—one there, another, then another—even they cannot keep me awake any longer.

November 3

It feels very strange, to think that we may be leaving all of this. But when I spoke with Hannah and Sadie and Jacob together on Sunday on the ride back home, it seemed very clear that this was the will of God.

Then when I woke on Monday, it felt much less clear.

To leave this behind, this place and this good sturdy house? With just two weeks of food, traveling across a land torn by famine and war? What sort of father would do that to his children? Perhaps I should speak against it.

I remember, again, that feeling. Looking into the cold empty eyes, and the raised barrel of that gun. Knowing that I would die, in that moment. It was not that knowledge, I think, that tightens the band around my heart.

It was Hannah, and Sadie, and Jacob. It was that I did not want what was coming for them, though I know it was not humble. I did not want them to fear, so I felt fear for them. I see that, out there, casting us again in the face of guns and the starving, wandering, desperate English.

I know that fear should not rule me. I know I should be open, to what it is that God is asking us to be. That we should submit ourselves. I know this. But I still do not want harm to come to my Hannah, to good-hearted Jacob, to my strange, bright Sadie.

And should we leave? Should we flee? I think of the old story of the Dutch Anabaptist Dirk Willems, fleeing his captors across the frozen ice. When his jailer broke through the ice, and cried out in the frozen water, did he leave him behind? No. He returned to help him, even though it meant his death.

But then I remember our own exodus to this country, to a place where we could live in peace, troubling no one. Which is God's path? To which should we give ourselves?

My heart is troubled, and again, I feel that tightness and uncertainty. I do not like this feeling.

I spoke this to Hannah, shared it with her in the late morning, when Shauna was out harvesting greens, and Mike and the boys were over helping some men from a neighboring farm get another combine running. I do not yet wish them to know that this journey is being planned.

"Oh, Jay," she said. "It frightens me, too. For Sadie and Jacob, and for all of us. But I think it is what is meant to be."

And then she rested her hand on my shoulder, and folded in close, as she does sometimes when I need persuading.

"You are a good man, Jay. Go talk with Sadie. Go talk with her. Ask her."

And so I did.

She was done with her morning chores, and was out by the

graves of the boy and the man. She had brought the pants Jacob had torn through the other day, and my socks that needed darning. She was stitching them, quietly, by herself. Her sewing bag was by her side, as cluttered as always. She heard me coming, and glanced up, but went back to her needlework.

I sat beside her, and my knees cracked as I did.

"What is it, Dadi?" she asked. Her little smile, delicate as a flower on her slender face.

I told her what the men had said, what was being discussed. I told them they had talked about her, and she laughed.

"About me?"

I said yes, and she laughed again. It was a woman's laugh, like her mother's, but bright and young still. I saw her, now not a girl, not a child. It is hard to see who a person is, through all of those memories of who they were.

I told her what I was thinking, and I asked her what she thought was God's will in all of this. It was hard getting out the words, to ask my little bird such a thing. What father asks his child for advice?

But she was more than a child, now.

She looked away, her eyes soft and distant. "Some things God wills, and we cannot change. We cannot change the tides. Or a storm, on the earth, or on the sun. Or that I was born a girl. Or that you are my dadi. We are so small, and those things will happen whether we will it or not.

"But there are other things." She gave a little laugh. "Is it God's will that we leave?" Her eyes fluttered, then closed, and she spoke, almost to herself. "God knows what it would be for us to stay. And God knows what it would be for us to go.

If we stay? It would be like Derek, with that pistol of yours. We would live. Some of us. But it would be terrible. And the blood shed by the English would stain our hands."

Her hands busied with the sewing as she spoke, carefully, slowly. And then she paused, and her face turned up to me. "And if we go? Then the story of our journey will be told and remembered. Of our setting aside what we have, and not resting in the shadow of the sword. It will be harder. Some of us will not live. More, I think. But it would let us live our plain way, and be a witness."

Her eyes fixed on mine. They were as deep as the sky. "Which is God's will? Both. Neither. And the many ways between. There are so many ways in between."

I said that I did not fully understand.

"I don't either," she said, her voice soft and plain, still holding my gaze. "God's will is too big for me to see. It hurts to see even part of it. Like a fire. But I think it will be better if we go, and face the harder journey. More like Him."

And I knew what she meant.

She looked down, back to her sewing, and nestled back against me as she did. Like when she was a little girl.

We sat for a while.

Then she said, "Dadi?"

"What?" I said.

"I think your memories are hard, a burden. All that writing, of the terrible things. Maybe they are something you should—leave behind."

I gave a shudder, hearing my thoughts in her voice, and

heard the blood suddenly coursing in my ears. Her voice continued, softly.

"There will be enough hardship on the road ahead. Why carry the hardship of the past? Maybe you could leave your remembering behind, with the house and the barn and these bodies in the ground. Maybe in a new place, with new and empty pages, it will be better. You can write about the journey, and about the new place."

She sat in silence for another moment, and her hands stopped sewing.

She rummaged in her bag for a moment, and pulled out a notebook, simple and leather-bound. "I had Jon get it for you from the store. Not many people buying them, so it was free."

She placed the notebook in my open hands, and the wind played through the empty, half-open pages.

"But you do what is best, Dadi."

So. I was decided.

AND WHEN WE GATHERED together, that afternoon at the Schrock farm, I found that most had decided in the same way. Of the twenty-three families in the district, twenty-one saw God's will in our leaving. The two that did not chose to submit, and so we would all together leave.

The end of it, the certain end of it. Or the beginning of it.

Ah. It is late. I am not tired, but it is late! I must stop writing this now.

November 5

Jon passed through this morning, moving quickly. The news was from other settlements in the district, where the talk of exodus was everywhere. We would move on.

Of the one hundred and eighty-two districts, one hundred and fifty-seven had chosen to leave. Within two weeks, there would be thousands of us going westward, racing the winter. Young men without wives and children were volunteering to ride out ahead, to make contact with families and the bishops of those districts, to bear the message that we were coming.

"And you?" I asked.

Jon gave me a look. "And me?" he said. "Bishop Schrock asked if I can bear the tidings. I can travel much faster, carry a week's supplies."

I could see that this pleased him, young and strong as he was. I asked him what his mother and father thought of this, and he laughed.

"Someone's gotta do it. And who better than me? I'm the best rider in the district. They know that."

I smiled at him, and warned him not to be prideful.

He winked back. "It's not prideful. It's just true."

Halfway down the path to the road, Sadie appeared, carrying a basket full of potatoes still heavy with dirt. Jon gave me a nod, and cantered over to her.

They exchanged words, words that I could not hear. But I could see the look he was giving her. And I could see that she saw it, too. She handed him something, and he thanked her.

And he was off, riding a little faster than he'd come, faster than he needed to.

HANNAH AND I TOLD Mike and Shauna of our decision later in the morning. The four of us sat together after a late breakfast, after the young folk went to pick spinach and greens, and to continue harvesting the last potatoes. I knew it would not be an easy conversation, but it needed to be done, so I did it.

With Hannah at my side, I told them what we had planned, and why. And that we would leave them this place, and all of the stores we could not carry with us. It will be enough to carry you through winter, I told him. And you have learned enough from these weeks together, I told him, enough to do what you need to keep the farm.

I gestured to the shelf in the sitting room, by the kitchen, to where our books sat, neat and in a row. And there, I said, we will leave you books on farming. It will be at least a week before we are ready to begin the journey, and we can talk so that you can know everything you need to know.

And then I handed him the title for the house, and the document I had written up last night saying that he had the right to live here and care for the house in our absence. It included my signature, and Hannah's, and a place for him to sign.

"I do not think you will need this," I said, "because I don't know that there are many lawyers out plying their trade now. But just in case, if anyone asks, or if there's a problem. This is your home, for as long as you need it."

Mike was quiet, for a little, and Shauna sat with her hand pressed to her mouth, her eyes filling, dancing from Hannah to me and then back again.

Mike stood, and made a show of looking at the title and the document, but I could see that he was really staring at his feet. He did not look at me when he spoke. "Jacob, it's your home."

"I know," I said.

He uttered the Lord's name, but not in vain, I don't think. Then he took a deep breath, and let it out in a jagged, splashing exhalation.

"I know you folk do what you think you need to do. But from what I hear, from the men I've been patrolling with, things are just a total mess everywhere. There's just, I mean, it's, just . . . You're going out like lambs to the slaughter."

I told him that was God's will, not ours.

"I knew you'd say that," he replied. His voice was raised a little, with a tremble in it. "Look, it's amazing that you're just leaving all of this for Shauna and me and the boys, but you'll die out there. All of you."

I told him that might be so, but that it was not for us to decide.

He uttered a soft curse, then apologized for it. Shauna spoke, her voice unsteady.

"And I don't know what we're going to do without you. I don't know if, I mean, we just can't . . ." She trailed off.

"Of course you can," Hannah said, her voice soft and strong. "You will have this place. You will have food enough, and you are known to the community now. Come spring, the land will give what you want. And God will do with us what God wills."

And Shauna was crying, and Hannah was holding her.

"So that's how it has to be." Mike's voice, a little gravelly, his eyes meeting mine, then looking anywhere else.

"Yes," I said. And so he signed the paper, and Shauna did, too.

I suppose the conversation could have gone worse.

November 12

Hot again today. November, and it is so hot. But I am too busy to write. It is good, that I am too busy to write.

And better yet that I am too busy to read. This page is the only page I will let myself see today.

November 17

Got the horses shoed today, and finished the cover for our wagon. The cover is an old plastic tarp, bright blue, which must do. Though it looks silly.

We are almost ready. And I will not keep reading this. I will not.

November 19

I will write in this book, this one last time, about today, because it is the last day, and that seems worth putting down, even if the words are soon discarded.

This morning, the day broke clear and cloudless, and the first of the Plain folk from the settlement began to pass. A line of buggies, gray-topped and humble, black sides shining, like ants in a row on a kitchen floor. They cast long shadows.

Most were laden, not with people, but with bags and food and supplies. Mixed in were wagons, also laden with supplies. All around them, the people walked, the pace slow and unhurried.

We watched them pass, and waved, and shouted greetings to those we knew. Hannah and Sadie walked down to the road, and there were leave-takings and short prayers. I watched, as here and there some of the passing women would approach Sadie, and hug her, or offer her a prayer. Other women would just look, and others still would look but try not to be seen looking. The men would nod as they passed, silent recognition.

How much has changed.

But while Hannah and Sadie greeted, I went back to the barn. There was much to do. I have been working on both the buggy and the wagon these last few days, to make sure they are ready for the journey. We have preserves and water, dried meat and fruit, and a barrel of new potatoes, and squash and apples. It will be enough. It will have to be. Mike and the boys will help me load today, as will my Jacob.

We have clothes, what little we have, both for winter and summer. We will bring one of our milk cows, and the horses, of course. The horses are newly shod, and we have replacement shoes for them both. Other things we must find as we go will be grass enough on the way for them, and fuel for our cookfires.

I have chosen from my tools those most useful for the road, and for building or being of use when we reach our destination. Everything is ready.

Then there are the other things, the things we cannot bring, the things we do not need. We have chosen carefully and humbly, but some things were harder to leave. My lathes. So many of our books, though some come with us.

Not this one, though. Or the others in which I have written.

Dinner was a little sorrowful this evening, and Shauna cried a great deal as we talked of our parting. Afterward, we went outside, and in the cool of the dimming day, we looked out to the darkened skies. They are beautiful, so full of stars. The Milky Way, clear as can be. We stood together, and watched the skies come alive and dance with so many lights.

Now, I am done. We rest, in readiness for the morning.

And this book, this book? I will leave it now. I am done with them, these memories. The words of scripture sing in my head, "the past is finished and gone, everything has become fresh and new."

I will put it in this drawer, this drawer I fashioned with my own hands. I will close the drawer.

And in the morning, we will walk, with the sun like a shepherd behind us.

Acknowledgments

Rache, thank you for your wifely encouragement and good words of direction. Mom, Dad? Well. Obviously. Thank you for both bringing me into existence and for your support. Chuck and all the folks at Algonquin, thank you for your insights and your edits and your guidance. You have refined this into an infinitely better tale. Plus, you've published it, which still freaks me out a little bit. Kathleen, thank you for taking me on, and for having perhaps the most honey-buttered voice of any literary agent on the continent. The good souls at Poolesville Presbyterian Church, thank you for being the kind of church where a pastor is welcome to dream and create.

And Phyllis. Oh, Phyllis. Thank you. I wish you'd lived to see this in print. This book exists only because you took the time to make the way straight for it. I trust, from the faith we share, that this little story is known to you in some way I do not yet fully understand.